PHASE RIDER

A
LightLit®
Book

DAVID LEVIN

For information about this title or to order other books and/or electronic media, contact the publisher:
LightLit®
Houston, TX 77062
lightlit.online
davidllevin@aol.com

ISBN: 978-1-7338351-0-7 print
         978-1-7338351-1-4 eBook

Printed in the United States of America

Cover and Interior design: 1106 Design

This book is dedicated to Lissa Rae Sunseri,
a sweet soul without spot or blemish in heaven.

Other books by David Levin:

Promise

Teen Law

The Scruffy Series:
   The Demons of San Antonio (Book Three)
   Demon Dust (Book Two)
   Meatball Heaven (Book One)

Rue

Sine Qua Non

A Fracking Good Time

Thirteen billion seven hundred million light years from the Milky Way the universe caught fire. A horizon of energy grew into a towering tsunami consuming matter, energy, space, and time. The oldest galaxies, dim with dying stars, were the first to disappear, followed by clusters of galaxies. Super-massive black holes disintegrated in the inferno. The fabric of space-time was bent and contorted by gravitational waves that sent cosmic bodies crashing together to litter the universe with debris waiting to be destroyed. Countless worlds of intelligent beings watched in disbelief and horror as the conflagration consumed their planets. Attempts to escape in spacecraft of advanced technology ended in disaster. Debate concerning the demise of our universe concluded. The end of existence was at hand.

"The phase transition continues. It is headed toward us faster than the speed of light." Doctor Lewellen returned his attention from the small audience of scientists to the maelstrom depicted on the Deep Space Monitor. "These images are from our astronomer on Pluto, Whiteside. He's using the new advanced sensor telescope recently installed there."

Uneasy chatter rippled among the elite group of boffins assembled at Houston's Johnson Space Center.

"*Niet.* Nothing can exceed light speed, not even pure energy," Professor Bobrov said in a heavy accent. "Your instrument on Pluto must be defective."

"Quite so, Lewellen. I know Doctor Whiteside. He is a good man. However, his readings must be off, perhaps an anomaly from the new telescope not being calibrated properly," astrophysicist Lord Terrence Alcock said as he cleared his throat in proper British fashion.

"Gentlemen, as improbable as it may seem," Doctor Lewellen ran his hand across the screen of his smart phone, "this data is correct. No mistake. We have confirmed it by the advanced telescope as well as radio arrays on Mars and our deep-space satellites. Arecibo also agrees. There is simply no doubt about these conclusions. The phase transition is not merely approaching us. It distorts the entire fabric of space-time, collapsing some matter while pulling and stretching other matter, much the same as a tidal wave draws coastal water to it before smashing into land. We are witnessing nothing less than the destruction of our universe from its transformation into a new form of matter. Electromagnetic energy seems to be instantaneously transmitted from the transition boundary, thereby giving us real-time information. These pictures appear almost instantaneously as worlds and galaxies disintegrate. The result of quantum entanglement across vast distance, I believe."

A soft murmur ran through the assemblage before tailing off into nervous nothingness.

Lord Alcock cleared his throat again. "How long?"

"What difference does it make? Be strong, like us Russians. We will stand together and spit in its eye," Professor Babrov said with a snort.

"The monarchy, sir. I have a duty to His Majesty so that he may make preparations. British tradition and all. I am sure you understand my position." Lord Alcock averted his gaze to a window providing a view of Rocket Park and the throng of gawking tourists.

Doctor Chow hissed. "Tradition? Not much use for that now." He stood, walked to the monitor, and turned to Doctor Lewellen. "However, I would like to know as well. How much time for the last pleasures of life? Our party leaders also require that information. We will not alert the masses. That could lead to revolution."

"Eleven months, maybe shorter. Damned thing seems to be picking up speed," Doctor Lewellen answered.

"Should not we tell the world about this tragedy? Isn't that our duty as scientists, irrespective of politics?" Doctor Pierre Gaston asked. "We French believe in allowing people to live freely, as they choose. How can they do that if the people are not informed of what lies ahead? I, for one, will want to experience like's great pleasures one more time. French wine, a fine meal, the company of a beautiful woman."

"Impossible. Not everyone is as orderly as you French. Terror and chaos could result. Rather than pleasure, the remaining months of life might well turn into riots, looting, gang violence, the overthrow of authority. No, gentlemen, it is best to keep this news tightly controlled. We have experience with such matters in China," Doctor Chow said.

"How will it be for us, Lewellen?" Lord Alcock asked. "At the end, I mean. Will we suffer?"

"Perhaps, but not for long." Doctor Lewellen stood and rubbed the back of his neck. "Doctor Ayana theorizes that the transition results from negatively charged subatomic heavy-mass particles of unknown origin interacting with conventional nuclei of our universe. The result is a release of intense energy, X-rays primarily, and the transformation of normal atoms into new matter. Many could die from radiation poisoning. Others might perish from heat stroke. The lucky ones will lose consciousness before the end."

"Lucky? Our atmosphere and oceans will begin to evaporate first, I think," Professor Babrov said with a defiant stare at Doctor Lewellen. "That is why we must be strong."

"Gentlemen, let us adjourn for now. I will keep you informed of developments. Perhaps the phenomenon will slow." Doctor Lewellen returned his attention to the monitor.

The scientists quietly filed from the conference room, some chatting quietly, others in reflection, leaving Doctor Lewellen with troubled thoughts.

A melodious ring failed to distract him from his cerebrations. It persisted until he retrieved his cell phone and looked at the screen. It was an incoming message from Doctor Ayana: "Please call me as soon as possible."

Doctor Lewellen obliged, and the other party answered on the first ring. "Lewellen, thank God you returned my call. We must talk at once." Doctor Ayana seemed out of breath.

"My good friend. How is the foremost mathematician in the world? It brightens my thoughts to hear from you. Brings back fond memories of our graduate school days. I wish for them now."

"Happy to do that. But I have little time for polite talk, Lewellen. It is imperative I meet with you right away about the phase transition."

"Too late for theoretical science, Ayana. Your calculations are correct. We have confirmed that our universe is changing physical properties and being destroyed in the process. We just concluded a meeting about how much time we have left. Blasted thing is moving so incredibly fast. I have accepted that we are doomed."

"No, Lewellen." Doctor Ayana's voice became shrill. "I have discovered something that might help."

"What?"

"It results from my new work after our scientific meeting last month on the phase transition, but I cannot explain over the phone. Too many expressions and formulae. Can you meet with me tomorrow? There is a nonstop from Addis Abba to Houston tonight. I could be at your office in the afternoon. Will that work for you?"

Doctor Lewellen's silence caused an explosive plea from his friend. "We must meet at once! Please clear your calendar. The fate of humanity rests in our hands."

"All right, Ayana. I will cancel my meetings. Tomorrow then. Truth be told, I'm tired of all the scientific blather right now. It has given me a terrible headache."

Doctor Lewellen studied the vast amount of mathematical data that occupied six computer monitors: numbers, formulae, equations, expressions, and symbols. He scrolled down the last monitor as the data seemed to be never ending. "I recognize some familiar mathematics. Calculus, differential geometry, and linear algebra, mostly. But much of your work is unfamiliar. Some new math you have been keeping secret?"

The seven-foot-two-inch Ethiopian stood, towering over his colleague, and smiled, his large white teeth stark against ebony skin. "You noticed. That is good. When I decided on a scientific career rather than professional basketball, people said I was stupid. How unfortunate. I came to Houston as an undergraduate, played basketball, won two college championships, and everyone assumed that was all I could do. Yet, I knew better. Science was my passion, and I was good at it. All As in honor courses. A PhD, but they still ridiculed me for not taking the money and fame." Doctor Ayana slowly ran his massive hand over a monitor, caressing it as gently as he would a newborn. "This, Lewellen, is not the work of a stupid man. It is what I call Quantum Reconciliation, the mathematical accommodation of general relativity with quantum physics, scientific proof of the nature of existence across all lines of thought. The holy grail of physical laws."

"Why haven't you published this work? It could lead to something great."

"Such as some great prize, perhaps the World Scientific Gold Medal? I saw greater rewards than peer approbation. Preventing hurricanes, reversing climate change, capping volcanoes before eruptions." Doctor Ayana's eyes glazed over, as though he were in a daydream. "Lewellen, this new knowledge will allow us to travel across the cosmos, not in light years but in seconds, transform alien planets into worlds that will support humans, block solar storms, destroy incoming asteroids no matter how massive."

Doctor Lewellen blinked several times, reminding one of a camera taking successive images. "Are you saying that your mathematics can lead to unlimited power to change our universe?"

"The stuff of creation. And transformation." Doctor Ayana's eyes now were afire as he scrolled to the end of the data on the monitor. The final equation seemed deceptively simple, but profound: $Ex = (ME)^4T$. "This, Lewellen, is the answer, supported by all of the preceding data. Existence equals the total calculated mass of the universe, including dark matter, times the total energy of the universe to the fourth power times the temperature of the Big Bang at the moment inflation commenced."

Doctor Lewellen's voice was raspy. "Energy to the fourth root. Why?"

"My work conclusively proves that the fundamental forces of nature—gravity, electromagnetism, the strong nuclear attraction, and the weak nuclear attraction—were combined into a single overriding force at creation. Something that could expand matter beyond the speed of light. This force was accelerated by the immense temperature of the Big Bang's pure energy singularity."

"And this is true on a quantum level?" Doctor Lewellen's eyes had become as wide as those of a child peering through a candy store window.

Doctor Ayana winked. "Down to the quark."

"My God. If we can do that, and it is admittedly a big if, we could transform the universe." The potential of his words froze Doctor Lewellen in a catatonic-like state.

"I know. We just might be able to reverse the phase transition. That is why it was so urgent I meet with you."

Doctor Lewellen regained his senses and paced from monitor to monitor, glancing briefly at each one, until he said, "But how can we make this practical? Actually stop the cursed thing."

Doctor Ayana walked to the window and pointed. "Out there, in West Texas. The new ultra high energy laser operated by a partnership of universities, called the Texas High Beam." He retrieved a ballpoint pen from his jacket and touched the tip. "A small amount of diatomic hydrogen molecules fused by the laser into a new form of matter, according to my mathematics, to become an anti-transition element that will interact with the phase transition and cancel it out, much the same as with matter and antimatter." Doctor Ayana's forehead wrinkled as he retrieved his smart phone, his long fingers flying over the keys to do advanced math. Suddenly, he stopped and blinked at Doctor Lewellen. "We will, of course, need to deliver this element at precisely the correct point along the transition's leading edge to achieve an extinguishment."

Doctor Lewellen expressed a thought. "I hope Mission Control can get an unmanned craft close enough."

"Could be a problem, but I have to do more calculations to determine the precision needed." Doctor Ayana used his phone calculator and shook his head.

Doctor Lewellen swallowed. "Are you thinking that an astronaut will need to do it? What about the reaction, and radiation? Is it likely a human can survive?"

"I am afraid that only a highly skilled astronaut will do." Doctor Ayana breathed deeply. "The mission will require a human to get close enough to deliver the element precisely by confirming computer targeting. The transition boundary changes quickly, and our target will become apparent only at the last second. Our most advanced super computer can respond better than a human brain. However, radiation at that distance will penetrate any shielding and affect the computer's performance. Our pilot must be prepared to act if the computer fails." He stopped and swallowed. "After that, the entire craft will probably be destroyed. The reaction concussion . . . well, it will lag behind. Most likely, the craft will be incinerated by then. The mission requires someone who will knowingly face death to save our universe."

"At least it is possible." Doctor Lewellen's eyes became thin slits of mental focus. "We will need full government cooperation and all of NASA's resources, and those of our scientific partners, including the Russians. We can't be impeded by the bureaucrats. No time for their nonsense. I need to go to the top." He pushed a button on an intercom. "Mary, see if you can get the president. Tell her it's an emergency."

CHAPTER 3

The telephone rang in Colonel Thad Session's office at Area 51. He studied the caller ID information and retrieved the receiver. "General Jackson, what a surprise. You know how it is for us guys at Area 51. Nobody cares about us because we don't exist. To what do I owe the honor of this call from the director of NASA?"

"This is no time for jokes, Thad," the general sternly said. "I need your full cooperation as the commander of Groom Lake."

"Absolutely. We're at your disposal. I was kidding when you called. Just trying to get a rise from my old buddy, since you're a big shot now. What's up?"

The general did not take the banter bait. "Thad, I'm calling on behalf of the president."

The colonel sat straight up from a reclining position.

"She directed me to inquire about your efforts on the antigravity drive. What progress have you made? It's critical that we know," General Jackson said in a demanding manner.

"Our scientists and engineers have confirmed that the alien craft uses antigravity propulsion, and that it probably achieved the warp speed our physicists predicted, somewhere around ten times the speed of light."

"Are you able to reproduce the technology now?" General Jackson asked.

"Not as close to doing that as I'd like. We understand most of the propulsion machinery. But it's one last component that we're having trouble cracking. Some crazy vessel with turns and turns of tubes and wires. It could be a graviton harvester. We really don't know. Why are you asking?"

General Jackson responded gruffly. "Because we have a special mission in deep space and the president wants the fastest craft. Your antigravity drive is the best bet. It should beat even the antimatter engine, if you can tell us how to build one of the darned things."

"Okay, sorry we don't have full knowledge of it yet. We've been working hard on the project. How much time do we have to figure this thing out?"

"Look, Thad, I'm not trying to be heavy-handed and I apologize for being short with you. You were a hell of a good airman. But I need you to understand the immense pressure this mission has placed on us. I've got to put everything together as soon as possible. Time is very short."

"I do understand. Got no problem with the urgency. Can you tell me what the mission is about?" Colonel Sessions had fully recognized the seriousness of the matter.

"Wish I could, but the mission is top secret. I'm asking that you put every available engineer and scientist on the antigravity drive. If we can't get a functioning unit within about two months, then we'll have to go with the antimatter engine, and that will be much slower."

"I'll do that immediately. In fact, our best man, Doctor Grossman, just returned from sabbatical. He can lead the team. He's one of the top engineers in the country and a hard worker, a real bulldog. He'll go at the problem night and day."

"Let me know as soon as you have it solved. We'll then have to break a leg to produce a working prototype to test in our mission spaceship down in Houston."

"Yes sir. Our people will get on it today."

Colonel Sessions hurried from the office and got into his SUV. He drove beyond the posted speed limit to a windowless hanger built into the side of a rocky hill, where he used a radio in the vehicle. "This is Sessions. I need entry."

Massive double doors slid open allowing the colonel to drive into the cavernous structure. He continued past uniformed men and women working on two triangular craft of experimental design until he reached the chamber's end. A heavy round door in the hill rolled open to reveal a lighted road penetrating deeply into the earth.

He drove for two miles and stopped next to a concrete façade with a steel man door. The colonel faced an iris scanner.

"Access granted," it said.

Colonel Sessions walked into another hanger-like room. White-coated men and women attended a craft of unusual architecture: dull silver-colored metal skin forty feet wide and eleven feet high at the center, without aerodynamic features or windows, hovering silently above the concrete floor, in the shape of a saucer.

"Would you like to go inside, Colonel?" a young woman asked from underneath the craft. "We've made recent strides in understanding the instrumentation. Very interesting. Some eye-popping technology."

"I need to talk with you about the antigravity drive. The progress you've made on figuring out that last component. Got a minute for that, Doctor Ames?"

"You bet," she said as the woman walked toward him.

She searched notes on a clipboard and read for a moment before offering an explanation. "We ran a computer analysis on the component again. It definitely has to do with the antigravity drive. We haven't been able to determine whether it harvests gravitons or has some other function, such as increasing their energy. Our physicists just don't know at this time."

Colonel Sessions made eye contact. "We need to find out pronto. It seems NASA has some space mission requiring extreme velocity, and they think our antigravity engine can do the trick. The mission is waiting on us, and the NASA folks are breathing down my neck."

"*Our* engine?" Doctor Ames asked with a raised eyebrow.

"I know. Alien devices are in that craft." He gestured toward the flying saucer. "I merely meant it is entrusted to us to reverse engineer the spacecraft's technology, if we can solve the puzzle of this last component, that is."

"We're finishing a new program now. Advanced algorithms to run functional variations of the device based on design, components, and material. I should have some new information tomorrow or the next day. Let me check on that project right now."

"Of course. Thanks."

She moved briskly away and disappeared into another part of the structure.

Colonel Sessions walked around the craft, ran his hand over the smooth finish, and carefully tested the sharpness of the edge. He muttered, "What a piece of hardware. Like to have a fleet of these babies in our arsenal."

He left the craft and proceeded through another door and down an L-shaped hallway, stopping before a glass window manned by a uniformed military officer on the other side. "Afternoon, Lieutenant Killen."

"Afternoon, Colonel. Would you like access?"

"I would," Colonel Sessions responded.

"Very well. Access code, please," the lieutenant said.

"16764215 Milwaukee."

A door beside the window opened for Colonel Sessions. He proceeded down a hallway illuminated only by light strips in the floor. The end of the passage revealed another window through which he saw two dimly lit glass cylinders containing a green haze. Each held the body of a gray extraterrestrial biological entity, or ETBE as they were called, about seven feet tall with a spindly body and long, thin arms; webbed feet and hands; a small, lipless mouth in a deltoid head sitting directly on narrow shoulders; large almond-shaped eyes that seemed to peer through the glass; and no other facial features.

He studied one of the beings. "What is the secret of the antigravity drive? How does that last part work? I wish we could tap your brain, if you are still alive, that is. Sure wish our biologists could figure that out."

A flash of intense electromagnetic energy emanated from the cylinder. Colonel Sessions covered his eyes in an attempt to shield them, but the light had temporarily blinded him. He blinked several times and rubbed his eyes before sight began to return. The colonel glanced at his hands. He froze as his mind started convulsing information he had not known. Mental images of formulae, diagrams, numbers, circuits, and interactive segments as clear as pictures on a wall. Everything started moving, as though the parts of a puzzle were pulling themselves together in the finished product. Instantly the mystery component was clear to him. He knew, with absolute clarity, its function.

He whispered softly, his whispers soon rising to be excited utterances. "My God. You must be alive, and sent that information to my brain. Thank goodness you are a moral being who is willing to help us, even though you are trapped." He looked away for a moment to collect his emotions. "That last part, it's a converter. Changes gravitons into anti-gravitons. Reverses the electrical charge by changing polarization. That's what produces the repulsive effect from gravity. The ship makes its own fuel from the gravitons that flood the universe. Brilliant, absolutely otherworldly." The colonel's mind wandered for a moment until his excitement returned. "Got to get this information to Jackson immediately. That will prove our worth out here in the desert. Now we should be able to build the blasted engine. And, hopefully, satisfy the president."

He whirled around to run down the hallway, but something stopped the colonel and made him look at the alien once more. Its penetrating eyes were staring at him.

CHAPTER 4

General Jackson looked at each person, twenty in all, men and women, black, white, Hispanic, and Asian. They presented an interesting mixture of qualities: seriousness, intelligence, salubriousness, strength, and experience. Their blue uniforms sported NASA emblems and projected an image of formal power, the Unites States' space explorers.

He waited for a moment more before speaking, as a dramatic pause. The room was silent. Then his voice rose over the gentle flow of air from diffusers. "Ladies and gentlemen, you are here at the request of President Lucille Ballieu. She asked me, as the director of NASA, to represent her at this most important meeting. Please let me make clear this is a volunteer mission. There is a significant risk that the astronaut who undertakes it will not survive."

The general scanned his audience as polite silence soon was replaced by subdued prattle among the astronauts.

"Excuse me, General, but we have accepted the dangers of our profession. We risk our lives on each mission. What is different about this one?" Air Force Colonel Peter Moss asked with a serious expression.

"This mission is unique, not like anything we've done before or anything we're planning. This astronaut will travel at extreme velocity and will be exposed to intense radiation in excess of any levels encountered previously."

Colonel Moss said, "We successfully protected the crew from cosmic rays to Pluto and back. As for velocity, do you mean the new antimatter engine that is expected to reach fifty percent of light speed? I thought we had developed plasma shields to fend off micro meteors for that vehicle."

"This mission will travel much faster, many times the speed of light," General Jackson responded.

The audience erupted in a controlled cacophony. "Impossible. What about Einstein's cosmic speed limit? We can't exceed light speed. Mass becomes infinite at that velocity."

General Jackson held up a hand. "This mission will use the antigravity engine. Our scientists tell me it can reach ten times light speed."

"Antigravity engine?" Colonel Moss blurted in obvious disbelief. "Come on, General, no science fiction stuff. There is no such propulsion system. We would know."

Others chimed in with similar sentiments.

"I understand. No one outside of very few people knows of this technology. However, I can assure you it is real. We are testing a prototype now at Ellington."

Silence again gripped the audience.

General Jackson continued. "We expect the velocity of the craft, in this special case, to be much more even than ten times the speed of light. It stems from a distortion of the fabric of space-time. Somewhat like riding a hurricane-generated wave toward shore."

Colonel Moss said, "Yeah, and everyone knows that is a stupid thing to do. Only foolhardy thrill seekers ride storms."

General Jackson glared at the colonel. "This mission won't be about thrill seeking, Colonel. We must achieve extreme velocity to conclude the mission on time."

"I was just using your analogy, General, not making light of the mission." Colonel Moss seemed to focus on what the general was saying. "How can any spacecraft withstand the heat created from the enormous amount of energy needed to achieve such velocity? I understand work on the warp drive was halted because they couldn't solve the problem of destructive engine heat."

"This case involves different technology. There will be heat. However, the antigravity drive creates a bubble of space-time that will envelope the craft, much the same as a Pacific curl hides the surfer. I want to be completely honest, though. Whether our vehicle can withstand those pressures is unknown. Cosmic radiation, however, will be shielded. Other radiation will become a problem when the astronaut slows to perform the mission. Ionizing radiation from the target is expected to be intense. More than cosmic radiation, even gamma rays. There is no reasonable expectation that we can adequately protect the craft's interior."

"You mean this is a one-way mission. The volunteer is expendable," Colonel Moss said.

The general breathed deeply. "Yes. Before you make any decisions, please allow me to bring in the scientist who designed the payload the craft will carry. He can also tell you about the reason for this mission." He walked to the door, opened it, and extended his hand.

Doctor Ayana ducked as he walked through the doorway, smiling widely, an expression seemingly inconsistent with the dire news he would deliver to the astronauts.

After a short introduction, the mathematician said, "I assume you have been briefed about the cosmological event approaching our solar system."

Captain Francine Trace, a navy pilot, straightened her posture, glanced at General Jackson, and said, "Cosmological event? Coming toward us. Is that what this is all about, some asteroid that we should be able to vaporize with a thorium warhead? Seems you are being melodramatic."

Subdued laugher rippled through the astronauts.

The smile never left Doctor Ayana's face, though it narrowed somewhat. General Jackson's attempted response was truncated by the mathematician. "Pardon me, General. Please allow me to do better than a cryptic explanation," Doctor Ayana said. "The information I am about to give you is top secret and may not be shared with anyone outside this room, even your family members. I myself signed a secrecy agreement and am obliged to ensure that you are aware this information falls under the secrecy agreements each of you signed about our classified space operations." He waited to allow his admonition to sink in. "The approaching phenomenon is no asteroid or planet or star. It is essentially another universe, or, to be more precise, our own universe changing physical properties to become a new universe, similar to liquid water turning into ice. It is called a phase transition. In the process, our universe changes to the point of ceasing to exist as we know it. Different physical laws will prevail, and all life in our universe will perish. As this transition advances, it leaves behind atoms of different electrical properties and masses than the atoms of which we are made. Most likely, the transformed matter will coalesce into another big bang."

Captain Trace uttered a single word: "Oh." She hesitated in thought for a moment before continuing. "But, are you sure? I mean, why haven't astronomers around the world reported this?"

"Because only NASA's specialized telescopes on Pluto and in our deep space satellites can see the transition's signature. Earth-based optical and radio telescopes can't detect the electromagnetic radiation or gravity wave effects where the transition is located," General Jackson responded.

"Then, what is the point of talking? Is this some data gathering flight?" Lieutenant Mike "Boomer" Carson, a military test pilot, asked sarcastically. "Isn't this all a waste of time? I mean, why the hell are we discussing space missions? I'd like to finish my bucket list before I become a frozen mackerel."

"Would you feel the same way if it were possible to stop the phase transition, reverse it?" Doctor Ayana asked.

Lieutenant Carson lost his sarcasm. "I, I suppose not. But how is that possible?"

"A single ultra-heavy atom of new matter created by the high output laser operating at full power in West Texas. Tests indicate energies so intense we can fuse an entirely new element into existence." Doctor Ayana slowly scanned the astronauts' faces. "If my calculations are right, this element could reverse the phase transition. Change it back to our matter. It will be like a bone marrow transplant replacing diseased tissue with healthy."

Lieutenant Carson asked, "What is so difficult about hitting a target with a space probe? Wouldn't an unmanned vehicle with an advanced computer have that ability? Seems to me there is no need to risk human life."

"I had hoped to do that," Doctor Ayana said, "but my latest calculations indicate the payload must be delivered at exactly the precise point to be effective. The phase transition acts like an amoeba. Its edge undulates as it moves across our universe. For a sustained reversal, we must strike a distinct point of that edge so that the reaction vectors along the entire transition boundary. Otherwise, it will merely be absorbed. The mission requires human target confirmation to maximize our chances of success. And even then there is no assurance we will succeed. Much of the mission is based on theoretical science."

"What are the chances of success to reverse this phenomenon?" Colonel Trace asked.

Doctor Ayana hesitated, seemingly thinking, before he said, "Probably well less than 50 percent, even if everything goes perfectly. We're still calculating final numbers."

"And how far away is this phase transition now? I mean, how much of the universe will we need to cross to launch the element?" Lieutenant Carson asked.

"Right now it's beyond the Sombrero Galaxy, about thirty-three million light years away," General Jackson answered.

The gathering's attentive demeanor was punctuated by a smattering of curse words.

"Wait a minute." Lieutenant Carson stood and addressed his colleagues. "Isn't it obvious? We should let the thing get closer, maybe to the edge of our solar system, and then blast it. Seems stupid to go all the way across the universe."

Doctor Ayana's smile had left him. His massive jaw muscles bulged. "Sir, to allow the phase transition to come that close would mean certain disaster. It emits intense heat from X-rays that would sterilize our planet and all life in our colonies on Mars and Pluto. In addition, the heavy element will create an energy reaction beyond anything we have detected before in the universe, more than a hypernova or the collision of neutron stars. That, alone, would destroy all of the planets in our solar system. Tear them to shreds. This mission must be conducted as far from us as possible."

General Jackson rose and spoke more softly than was usual for him, as though to lighten the emotional load just laid on the astronauts. "Look, I know this is heavy stuff. But you are our best and bravest. The most highly trained pilots in our country's history. That is why we turned to you. Our leaders have an incredible amount of trust and respect for each one of you." He forced a disingenuous smile. "Why don't you think about the mission and let me know tomorrow morning whether anyone would care to volunteer. And remember, they will probably name a school after the astronaut who does."

His attempt at humor seemed lost on the glum-faced space explorers who sat obviously stunned in silence.

CHAPTER 5

Doctor Ayana dialed a number on his cell phone and smiled when a man's voice said, "Ayana, you old rascal. I was thinking about you. Well, really, about the time when we played basketball together here and won those championships. Great time. What's going on with you these days?"

"Jessup, I hoped you would answer and not be at some important medical conference lecturing on genetics. After all, a PhD with your research credentials is widely sought after. I'm in town for a bit and hoped you might have time for dinner. Reminisce about our good old college days."

"You caught me between conferences, Ayana. Love to."

"How about going to the Safari Club? I have privileges there, and, besides, they have the best water buffalo bone-in filet. At least the one in London does," Doctor Ayana said.

There was a pause, prompting Doctor Ayana to ask, "That a problem? If so, we can do something else."

Doctor Jessup quickly responded. "No, nothing like that. The Safari Club is fine. I was just thinking that I'd like to show you something. The result of our applied genetics work." Doctor Jessup laughed. "I'm very happy with the result. We haven't published yet. I'd like you to be one of the first to know."

"Sure. Why don't you pick me up at the Regency?"

"Will do. Six o'clock be okay? I'm in a white Tahoe."

"Six p.m. then. Outside the lobby," Doctor Ayana said.

Bright Lighthouse was quiet. Several residents sat blankly before a muted television, its flashing images projecting various hues on their faces. One rocked back and forth involuntarily. A small group puzzled over toys and stuffed animals, seemingly incongruous for adults, until the observer realized they were afflicted with Down syndrome.

The absence of human conversation had an unpleasant quality created by caretaker dereliction of duties overseeing the wards in favor of the attendants' personal interests. The facility director was not present to hold staff accountable.

A resident broke the silence as he moaned in pain. "Please let me go, Mr. Anthony. You're hurtin' my arm. Real bad."

"I told you no poopin' in your pants. You need to tell me when you got to go." A large white-coated man gripped the resident's wrist.

"Sorry. It just came out."

The man raised a hand as though to strike the resident, until someone said, "Why are you doing that, Mr. Anthony? Don't you know it's against the law to hit a special-needs person?"

Anthony turned to face a short young man with a round face having oriental features. He smiled and said, "Why don't you let me clean him up, Mr. Anthony, so you can help some of the others?"

Anthony mocked him. "Oh, and I suppose you think you are so damned smart since that experiment. Listen, retard, I don't take no orders from you. Makes me no never mind what them doctors done, you still got Downs and that makes me smarter'n you. Got it, Mr. Bobby Smarty Pants Alderson?"

Bobby spoke calmly. "I agree with you, Mr. Anthony. Just trying to help with your chores. So things will be easier for you. Is that okay?"

Anthony hesitated, blinked, and said, "Yeah. Go ahead. Clean him up. Fine with me. I get so mad sometimes. Retards never can do nothin' right."

"I completely agree, sir," Bobby said with a sanguine expression as he led the soiled resident to a nearby bathroom.

Anthony snorted and left the room.

He exited the building and lit a cigarette on the front porch.

A female attendant joined him. "Got one for me?"

Anthony provided a smoke, and she took several drags until she said, "I swear, if that stupid monkey spills her drink again I'm gonna hit her where it don't show."

"Know what you mean, Liz." Anthony began to laugh.

"I don't see nothin' funny about them morons," Liz said through a puff of smoke.

Anthony glanced around and whispered, "That Sammy Jo. I hate her. All that jibber jabber makes me crazy as hell." He sneered. "But I got her good. Stupid retard. Hit her in the stomach to make her stop. She did, real quick. They thought she had a stomach ache." He laughed again.

A white Tahoe pulled to a stop in the parking lot.

Anthony sneered. "Damn. It's that doctor again. Peepin' in on us all the time. Wish he'd just go away."

"What doctor?" Liz asked.

"He worked on Bobby to make him smarter or somethin'. It's stupid. He's still a retard. Waste of good money."

Doctor Jessup and Doctor Ayana chatted as they entered the room where Bobby Alderson was playing with an autistic child.

Bobby noticed Doctor Jessup, smiled widely, and gyrated across the room like a bouncing ball. He hugged the visitor. "Thank you for coming. I missed you, Doctor." Bobby hugged him again.

Doctor Jessup held Bobby at arm's length to look at him with affection. "Good to see you, my friend. How is school coming along?"

"Great. An A in every class. English composition, calculus, physics. Honor roll again." Bobby beamed, his full cheeks matching a rotund physique.

"Bobby, I want you to meet a friend from Africa. This is Doctor Ayana, one of the smartest mathematicians in the world."

Bobby's eyes climbed Doctor Ayana, seeming to consider the man vertically, until he locked eyes, mouth agape. "Wow, you're the tallest person I have ever seen. Are you from the Tutsi tribe? I read about them. Real big people."

Doctor Ayana chuckled. "No, actually I'm one of the Oromo in Ethiopia." He patted Bobby's shoulder. "You seem especially well informed. I wouldn't think many youngsters your age would know that the Tutsi are some of the tallest inhabitants of Africa."

"I like reading, especially about different countries. People are interesting."

"Indeed. Do you read a lot?" Doctor Ayana asked.

"Every day. In school. After school, too." Bobby stood as tall as his compact frame would allow. "I go to Washington High School. Honors classes. We read a bunch. To learn all the advanced stuff."

Doctor Ayana glanced at Doctor Jessup in a curious way.

"Well, Bobby, I just wanted you to meet my friend, especially since you are so interested in mathematics," Doctor Jessup said.

"Terrific. I do like math. Looking forward to advanced calculus. Will we be doing any more stuff together, Doctor Jessup?"

"Yes we will, Bobby. We're finished with the shots, but I'll keep visiting to do some more tests. Is that okay with you?"

"You bet. I like tests. Since I do good on them now." Bobby smiled at his benefactor. "Thank you, Doctor." Bobby hugged the man, like a son shows love to his father.

The two scientists rode in silence toward the Safari Club, until Doctor Ayana asked, "How did you do it? That boy seems to have a normal IQ though he is obviously afflicted with Downs. Isn't that what you wanted to show me?"

"Yes. Bobby was left at a fire station, probably because of his birth defect. Essentially he's an orphan. He was sent to Bright Lighthouse as a baby. He's lived there with other special-needs kids ever since." Doctor Jessup stopped at a red light and looked at his passenger. "Then came the chance, Ayana. To test our new protein on a human being after years of research. All the wrangling for money paid off. Oh, the government basically turned its back on us. Only provided a trickle of funds. But a wealthy benefactor gave the real money we needed. Then, after our early tests, we were ready for a human trial. I was totally convinced that our protein was safe and could reverse Downs." The light turned green, but the Tahoe remained stopped as Doctor Jessup continued to explain. "The FDA gave us the go-ahead, and his guardian agreed. Six shots, that's all it took, just six injections." Doctor Jessup gazed in silence at the instrument panel, held by some powerful notion, until his words gushed. "And it worked, Ayana. Bobby's brain changed. His IQ rose from sixty to one hundred thirty-six, in the gifted range, within a matter of weeks. We disabled the extra copy of chromosome twenty-one, which causes Down syndrome. All this happened about five years ago when he was thirteen. After that we put him in public school, and he caught up with the other kids really fast. Now he's a senior planning on college next year. He even earned a full academic scholarship."

A honk caused Doctor Jessup to check the rear-view mirror and accelerate from the intersection.

"What about other Downs characteristics, such as health problems?" Doctor Ayana asked.

"It's too early to tell. Of course, physical features don't change. They are set. Basic personality traits as well. That's good because most Downs kids are sweet and loving." Doctor Jessup reflected for a few moments before saying, "Bobby is so concerned about others, almost altruistic. I am told by some of the Bright Lighthouse staff that he likes helping other kids there. Sure hope that doesn't change. The world needs more altruism and less arrogance."

Doctor Jessup's thoughts raced from this miracle of biology to its dizzying implications for the future of humanity. What great minds and selfless souls waited for release to bring peace, freedom, and healing to suffering people throughout a troubled world?

CHAPTER 6

The mood in the Johnson Space Center conference room was not somber, though facial expressions and body language might have said otherwise. Rather, it reflected exhaustion brought on by a catharsis of anger and sharp verbal exchanges.

Doctor Lewellen shook his head. "I can't believe that not one astronaut volunteered, not even any of the cosmonauts. And I thought the Russians were so tough."

"Can you blame them?" Doctor Ayana's powerful voice became a murmur. "We gave everyone a death sentence. Who would not want to live as fully as possible, spend every moment with loved ones, have that last sip of wine or bite of cake? And the extremely low probability of success may have sealed our fate of not getting a volunteer." Doctor Ayana reflected for a moment. "What about a military pilot?"

"Not that many of them left. Most of the fighters are drones these days. Those pilots are a dying breed."

"I wasn't aware of that development," Doctor Ayana said.

Doctor Lewellen whispered. "It hasn't been publicized, to keep our enemies guessing." He sighed. "Perhaps we approached the astronauts with the wrong message. Maybe we could have done better. But, I suppose the president was right not to inform the public. Even if that means missing some talented civilian pilot. Better to let the people live without depression until the end. Enjoy life as much as possible." He peered wistfully at a picture of Orion and asked, "Ayana, what do you think of super heroes?"

"Super heroes? You mean like the comic book characters children adore? Funny time to talk about pretend saviors. But perhaps not, if it makes you feel better."

"I was thinking about extraordinary bravery and selflessness. A hero's devotion to humanity. That is the kind of real-life person I am referring to."

General Jackson entered the room, followed by another uniformed man. "Are you ready for our teleconference with President Ballieu?"

Doctor Lewellen gestured that he was in agreement.

"I'll put us through now." The general used a remote to activate a wall-mounted monitor. It showed an empty desk for several seconds, until a woman seated herself behind the desk. Her flowered dress, sweet smile, and curly gray hair portrayed more a grandmother than a politician.

The woman's soft voice matched her appearance. "Gentlemen, thank you for taking the time to meet. I know you must be quite busy right now."

"It is our privilege, Madame President," General Jackson politely said. "Doctors Lewellen and Ayana are present, the leading scientists on this project."

"Very well. I have read your report on the approaching phase transition phenomenon and of the possibility of saving our civilization. However, I also read your memo this morning, General, about none of the astronauts volunteering for the mission. Does that scrub it or is there another way to proceed?"

"May I address that matter a bit later in our discussion?" General Jackson asked.

"By all means. This new element you described in the report, how soon can you have it ready to use for this mission? Sounds like quite a scientific undertaking to produce something entirely new to science."

General Jackson gestured toward Doctor Ayana, who said, "We have done our scientific work to create the new element. The only thing that remains is to produce this element using the Texas High Beam. It reaches extremely intense temperatures capable of fusing hydrogen atoms. That will require no time since the High Beam has been cleared to run at full power. The new element could be created and delivered to Ellington in a day. It would take two more for placement in the neutron projectile."

"General Jackson, is your spacecraft ready for launch?"

"Within days, Madame President. Capacitors can be fully charged with gravitons in thirty-six hours. The quantum computer is programmed and operational."

"How far is it to the phenomenon?" she asked.

"The phase transition boundary is just beyond the Sombrero Galaxy. About 33,000,000 light years from here," Doctor Ayana answered.

"Thirty-three million light years." The president was obviously surprised. "My word. How can any spacecraft cover such a distance in time to save us?"

Doctor Ayana took a piece of printer paper and penciled one circle at the top edge and another at the bottom edge. He held the paper up. "Madame President, if I may. Think of our universe like this. The Milky Way is here." He pointed to the top circle. "And the Sombrero is far away, here." Doctor Ayana touched the lower circle. "You are correct. Thirty-three million light years is a very great distance even for the most advanced propulsion technology."

Doctor Ayana grasped the paper in one hand for a moment, then crushed it. "This is what is becoming of the fabric of space-time. Distances are meaningless. Travel time is greatly distorted, shortened by orders of magnitude. It is similar to a hurricane churning up the sea into great waves and powerful currents. Travel on a sea like that is abnormal. The winds can hurtle a ship along much faster than its engines could. With the right navigation, we calculate that our vehicle can reach the transition boundary in as little as twenty-six days."

"Twenty-six days. Is that certain, Doctor?" she asked.

"Absolutely, so long as the cosmic forces remain distorted as they are now and as projected from the effects of the advancing phase transition," Doctor Ayana responded.

"Well, that is heartening. However, I would like now to address the piloting of our spacecraft. Since we had no volunteers for the mission, is there a reasonable chance of success? I understand you recommended a manned mission. Therefore, do you believe an unmanned craft has any realistic probability of stopping the phenomenon?" the president asked.

Doctor Ayana was amped up in explanatory mode. "We believe that a computer can navigate space but will have difficulty responding accurately to extreme cosmic conditions near the target. Scientists simply have no experience with such a situation. Therefore, we lack sufficient data for the computer to use in dealing with these circumstances." He paused in reflection for a moment. "There is also another factor. Radiation will increase as the craft slows near the transition boundary, to the point that the craft's shield will not be able to resist it. The radiation probably will affect the computer. To what extent is not known. The computer may fail before launching our projectile. The probability of an unmanned mission delivering the heavy element to the precise target we need is about 16.9 percent. A human may do better."

"You mean, launch the element with precision after the computer fails and just before he dies. Is that the reality, Doctor Ayana?" President Ballieu showed an acumen hidden by her grandmotherly visage.

"Yes." His voice was soft, almost apologetic.

She did not hesitate. "All right. Sixteen point nine percent is pretty slim, but at least it's a chance. Shield the computer with your most protective material, then program it with our best data. Produce the element as soon possible and get it to Ellington the next day. General, I would like to set launch for two weeks from today. Is that doable?"

"Yes, ma'am," he said.

"Then let's go to work. And gentlemen, please listen carefully." She seemed to wait for full attention. "No strong-arm tactics to force someone to do this mission. We will strive to succeed with the most advanced machine we have and pray for success."

President Ballieu ended the communication and immediately placed a call to the president of Russia on the hot line between the two antagonists.

A woman's voice answered in perfect English. "President Petrov's office. May I help you?"

"This is Lucille Ballieu. I need to speak to President Petrov, please."

A heavy Russian accent came across the line. "Mrs. President, so good to hear from you. Any news on our secret project?"

"Yes. That is the reason for my call. I just completed a review of final preparations for the spacecraft. The heavy element should be onboard and operational in three days. We plan to launch two weeks from today. Travel time is about twenty-six days. Of course, it would have been better if one of our astronauts had volunteered, but we will do our best with an unmanned mission."

"I will make a cosmonaut volunteer, if that is what you wish." His tone was gruff and forceful.

She spoke softly to calm the man. "Oh no, Mr. President. An unwilling pilot would not be in our best interest. Don't you agree?"

"Yes, but we Russians have our own special ways."

"I understand. However, an unmanned mission still has a chance of success. We are using the latest technology."

His tone mollified. "Excellent. I assumed your engineers would expect success. That is why I entrusted the mission to your country. This is no time for national posturing. We must be realistic and proceed with the most brilliant scientific minds."

"Thank you for the trust, Mr. President. We will do our best."

"Mrs. President." The Russian hesitated, as though considering his next words. "If the mission fails, have you any plans for the final months of life? How you call, the bucket list."

"Yes. I plan to spend them with my grandchildren in Lakeway. That is in the Texas hill country. We have a lake house there. My family loves that place. I can make it my second White House, much as Lyndon Johnson did with his ranch near Johnson City. I think we can still keep the matter secret to avoid mass panic. I will pretend to be on an extended vacation. Project a happy face. And you?"

"I will be at my villa on the coast of the Black Sea. Beautiful setting. Very restful for me. I will have the best caviar, Cohiba *Esplendidos,* single malt Scotch, and women." He laughed. "Yes, the most beautiful Russian women."

President Ballieu swallowed. "Indeed." She quickly changed the subject. "It is well we agree on not releasing this news to the public. I don't think that would be wise."

"We Russians have a saying, Mrs. President. Better to keep the bear calm, even if you must feed him vodka."

A mental image of a smiling bear changed her mood. President Ballieu's chuckle was overcome by his belly laugh, until he said, "And if we are successful, then we can announce to the world our accomplishment. Your people will love you, leading to a second term. My people, well, perhaps they will build a statue of me alongside that of our beloved Lenin."

The land outside of Van Horn, Texas, was flat, expansive, and covered with desert vegetation. Its hot, dry climate was more suited to rattlesnakes and horned toads than to livestock. Yet, this place had one very important quality to lure the Texas High Beam project: miles and miles of uninhabited range. The world's most powerful laser was housed underground in a reinforced concrete, ceramic-lined, circular tunnel two miles in circumference. The design was intended to contain a breach of the magnetic inner pipeline. However, for a column of light that had reached 7,000,000,000,000 degrees Celsius, more even than the Large Hadron Collider, scientists had acknowledged that the tunnel could not contain such vast energy. At least, they hoped the laser would not destroy any inhabited area before it was powered down. The beam's energy came from a mile square cluster of advanced solar panels generating enough electricity from the intense West Texas sun to run a mid-sized city.

Doctor Ayana studied a computer screen in the Texas High Beam control room before doing calculations on his smart phone.

"Doctor, are you ready for the tour?" Secretary of Defense Clarisse Brisbane asked after entering the room with three uniformed military officers and two white-coated women sporting badges that identified them as physicists Doctor Helen Clendenin and Doctor Patrice Mansfield.

"Yes, just let me finish this. I want to confirm the required atomic weight once again." He did more math and stared at the screen. "Third time. Just the same. Four hundred eleven. That is our atomic weight," Doctor Ayana said.

"You mean the weight of all protons and neutrons in the nucleus?" Secretary Brisbane asked.

"Yes, but it must also be stable. With a half-life of more than mere seconds. Enough to deliver the element to the transition. That is the key. We can always make elements heavier than naturally occurring Uranium 238. However, they decay in milliseconds to several seconds. No good for this work."

Doctor Clendenin said, "Very true, Doctor. But we have had difficulty in reaching the zone of nuclear stability."

"Exactly. That is why I dropped everything else to work on the details of this project. It is not just fusion that must be achieved. We must also maintain the reaction long enough to produce a usable half-life." Doctor Ayana smiled widely, as though about to disclose some incredible secret. He stared squarely Doctor Clendenin. "It is all here." He pointed to his smart phone. "The math tells us what we must do."

"I would like to hear the details. But why don't we go on the tour now? Our technical meeting will follow," the secretary said.

The group settled into golf carts inside the tunnel and proceeded along a concrete pathway adjacent to a gleaming, white, thirty-six-inch pipe that disappeared in the distance.

Doctor Mansfield narrated. "The beam is produced inside this pipeline, which is level to one thousandth of an inch. Computer activated adjusters keep it in that alignment."

She stopped the cart and pointed. "Carbon monoxide is placed in that vessel. It is contained there by electrostatic repulsion because the gas is extremely corrosive. We electrify the gas to produce plasma. The plasma creates an intense beam of light that is reflected into a two inch by eight foot ruby rod." She nodded toward a white box. Her arm swept the arch of the pipe. "The laser output from the ruby rod is then amplified many-fold through the principles of quantum mechanics. I will explain further at our meeting later."

Her cart led the others along the pipeline as she explained specialized equipment and certain design features. They ended the tour and convened in a conference room.

"I realize each of us has signed a secrecy document under the Espionage Act, but please allow me to reiterate this technology is top secret. It must remain under our sole control." Secretary Brisbane made eye contact with each person. "Doctor Mansfield, please continue."

Doctor Ayana raised a hand. "Excuse me, but did you say the laser is from a ruby? There is nothing unusual about ruby lasers. Aren't they widely used? How is yours different?"

"You are correct that ruby lasers are common." Doctor Mansfield peered over the top of thick glasses. "It is the photon harvesting that is an innovation, the secret technology."

"Photon harvesting?" Doctor Ayana wrinkled his forehead.

Doctor Mansfield took an erasable marker and drew a sketch: one small circle at the bottom of the board, a triangle just above that, two cylinders above the triangle. Next she drew one dotted line from the circle to the triangle and a dotted line from the triangle to each cylinder. Doctor Mansfield darkened one cylinder and said, "In quantum mechanics we know that a photon of light can become two identical bundles of energy." She motioned toward the drawing. "Here, a photon, represented by the circle, moves through a prism, which refracts the original photon into two photons. Each new photon then passes through a quartz cylinder. Though the photons are separate they are entangled according to the laws of quantum mechanics. They enter the quartz cylinders at the speed of light. However, while they are in the cylinders things change. We slow down one photon due to its cylinder being made of smoky quartz. The coloring minerals in that cylinder interfere with the photon's rate of travel. At this point the slower photon tries to catch up by expending energy. We harvest the slower photons as a secondary beam of light in a magnetic-walled pipeline."

Secretary Brisbane took up the explanation. "While other countries have tried to achieve ultra-high laser outputs with intense sources of light, we have reached more extreme temperatures with this approach."

"Pardon me, Madame Secretary, but why not use the main beam? Isn't it more energetic since those photons are traveling faster?" Doctor Ayana waited for a response.

"May I?" Doctor Mansfield asked. "You see, the harvested energy possesses a special property." She held up one finger, then extended two fingers of the other hand. "Energy being expended by the harvested photons to catch up with their twins causes the slower photons to double over time, so long as the main light source remains on. One bundle of energy becomes two, two become four, and so on, until the secondary beam is many times more powerful than the main beam."

"Light so intense it can excite atoms to velocities capable of fusing elements into exotic matter," Secretary Brisbane said.

Doctor Ayana stood. His vertical frame was taught. He grasped the marker, drew a circle containing several dots with arrows outside of them pointing to the center, turned, and said, "At 7,216,000,000,000 degrees Celsius, I calculate that we can create the heaviest artificial element known, at an atomic weight of 411. Fusion time must be very precise." He powered up his smart phone and scrolled through several screens of data. "Yes, here it is. One hundred and sixty-nine milliseconds. That is our fusion time for a stable element to reverse the phase transition. Are you sure the laser can maintain temperature for that period of time? I promised the president we would have the heavy element ready in one day. There is no time for trial and error."

Doctor Mansfield smiled.

The Ellington Space Port bustled with uniformed personnel attending a gleaming pyramidal craft resting on the launch pad. Its sides glowed a faint blue, the result of embedded Lominum crystals harvesting gravitons from dark energy. The gravitons were stored in supercooled magnetic capacitors for use in the antigravity drive. The craft's design lent itself to travel both in atmospheres and in the vacuum of space. This design also allowed a plasma shield to flow evenly over the surface to divert space dust and micro meteors away from the spacecraft.

General Jackson watched launch preparations in Mission Control at the Johnson Space Center only a few miles away. "Report on quantum computer checks."

"Sequencing completed. Data transmission, processing speed, memory all in the green," a flight engineer said.

"Graviton charge?" the general asked.

"Ninety-nine percent," another engineer answered.

"Launch window?" General Jackson turned toward a young woman.

"Open until eighteen thirty hours," she said.

An aide interrupted. "General, it's the president."

"Put her on the monitor," he ordered.

A large screen transitioned from a view of the spacecraft to a picture of President Ballieu seated in the Oval Office. "General Jackson, how are the launch preparations going? Are we on schedule?"

"Everything is a go, Madame President. We are waiting for 100 percent graviton charge," General Jackson said as he checked a computer screen. "That should be in one hour and ten minutes. Then we can launch."

"And the computer, is it fully programmed with our best scientific and observational information to deliver the payload as required for success?" she asked.

"Yes. Professor Carponi and his team have provided the latest data based on the most recent astronomical observations and deep space probe information. They also gave us various expected scenarios beyond the capacity of our sensors, and then pronounced their part of the programming ready."

"Have you also input all theoretical data, so that the computer will have as much information as possible on which to make decisions? Even if some of that information is our best educated guess at this time."

"We have, ma'am. Professor Whiteside at our Pluto observatory transmitted his latest theorized cosmic information. Space-time distortions, magnetic anomalies, gravitational waves, orbital perturbances, and his calculations of changes in those phenomena over the next month. He is one of the foremost astronomers, and we have great confidence in his work," the general said.

"Very well. Please keep me informed. The national science council is on standby to convene by teleconference while the mission proceeds. As you know, there is significant uncertainty among the members about an unmanned vehicle's ability to be successful. They want to review all data as it becomes available, and, I think, some of my critics on the council would like to tell me I was wrong in even attempting the mission." President Ballieu sighed. "Politics," she mumbled with a shake of her head.

"We will do that, ma'am. Doctor Ayana has calculated flight time at six hundred ninety-six hours and thirty-nine minutes based on current cosmic distortions." General Jackson hesitated for a moment. "We should know shortly after that."

"You mean whether or not the vehicle reached the transition boundary intact?"

"Yes, Madame President. But also whether your critics were right, or we saved the universe."

"I don't mind being wrong, General, or even facing criticism. Politics, however, are like brownies without sugar—distasteful. I do care very much about the people on earth. We must be successful for them."

"We will do our best, ma'am." General Jackson glanced at the countdown.

The screen returned to a view of the spacecraft.

"Turn off Lominum crystal harvesting until the ship reaches earth orbit. We want to remain in stealth mode," he said.

The countdown reached zero, and the pyramid disappeared in the blink of an eye.

An azure blur sped across the cosmos, propelled by antigravity technology enhanced by gravitational undulations. Navigation was by constant updating of star charts, possible only by a quantum computer capable of processing billions of calculations per second. The distortion of space-time had caused gravitational lensing that rendered conventional space navigation obsolete, much as light is bent away from its source when viewed through the base of a wine glass.

It had been six hundred ninety-five hours and fifty-eight minutes since launch. The spacecraft had successfully navigated around asteroids, black holes, neutron stars, magnetars, red giant stars, supergiant stars, and quasars. The computer had proven itself capable of safely crossing the dangerous cosmos. However, the final challenge lay ahead: correctly calculating the target and delivering the element precisely to that point along the constantly changing phase transition boundary.

The blur cleared as NASA's pyramidal spacecraft slowed on approach to a line of blinding energy that stretched across the universe. The line pulsated and moved as though alive, at times reaching toward the craft and then receding at seemingly unimaginable speed. The craft came to a stop, its sensors scanning light years across the transition boundary. The Quantum 1000 calculated countless data points: energy spikes, radiation bursts, cosmic winds, magnetic anomalies, gravitational waves, boundary shifts, distance changes, matter and antimatter reactions. It detected showers of fermions, quarks, leptons, bosons, hadrons, baryons, gluons, and mesons, as though the guts of the universe had been sliced open to spill out its contents.

Radiation levels rose in the craft despite the plasma shield that had protected the craft through deep space. The Quantum 1000 recorded elevated amounts of gamma rays, X-rays, cosmic rays, and charged particles breaching the protective shield. A computer paroxysm flashed on the main monitor: "Warning; electronic circuits will soon fail from radiation overheating; heavy element must be deployed within thirty-three seconds, before total system collapse."

A hatch slid silently into the wall of the craft's leading side revealing a glowing sphere. The Quantum 1000 calculated, read sensor data, hesitated, and recalculated the target once again.

The phase transition seemed to parry the computer's calculations, as if it were some omniscient entity changing shape to defeat the attack.

At thirty-one seconds since the warning, the Quantum 1000 sensed increasing radiation levels penetrating the craft and could wait no longer. It released the sphere concomitantly with the computer's circuits overheating and melting.

The projectile sped toward extinction's advance, carrying the hopes of observers in the earth's solar system.

CHAPTER 7

Doctor Lewellen concluded his observations and turned to General Jackson with hands clasped and resting against the scientist's lips, preferring to think before saying, "It appears the phase transition continues to advance toward us. Our element did not stop it." He rubbed his forehead with one palm.

General Jackson cursed. "I thought the heavy element would work. The president as well. What do I say to her? That our best minds couldn't get the job done? That we have no idea what we're doing? Damn disgrace for our geniuses, for us all." He cursed again. "Guess I will just have to be the one to tell her. I'll make Ayana be on the call with me. He's the one who came up with the idea. I think he should take some of the heat."

"It wasn't the element, at least as far as we know," Doctor Lewellen said.

"What then? And so what? A failure is a failure. We're going to die, plain and simple."

"The computer crashed. Sent out a death knell due to intense radiation around the time it launched the element. It probably needed more time to get a fix on the target before the circuitry burned up." Doctor Lewellen shrugged. "But radiation may not have been the only problem.

The computer could have had trouble handling all the rapid changes in space-time near the transition boundary. Much too chaotic there, like the environment around a black hole. It appears that no unmanned mission can do that job, at least with our current computing technology. Whiteside confirmed from his observations the massive cosmic turbulence in that region of space. I'm not even sure our best astronaut could hit the target." He looked at the floor. "Maybe an extraordinarily capable human could. But it would have to be someone able to remain calm while willingly sacrificing his life."

"No human is brave enough to volunteer. I know. Looked the cowards right in their eyes. Makes me sick to my stomach," the general said as he clenched his teeth. "If we could use just any trained pilot, I'd volunteer. But I get it. This mission requires someone with exceptional skill not generally found even in jet jockeys like me. A person selected for a unique talent to direct a vehicle through recurring dangers to a precise point. Someone probably not even in the astronaut program."

"They're not cowards, General, only normal people wanting to live what is left of their lives in meaningful ways, like being with their families." Doctor Lewellen stopped and reflected, before saying, "That's probably why they wouldn't succeed anyway. Because they are so normal. As you said, this mission requires an unusually gifted human being. Someone completely selfless, with a special intellect and incredible navigational skills. And there is something else to consider."

"Yeah, what's that?" General Jackson asked.

"Whiteside said things are getting even worse. Space-time is literally collapsing onto itself. Even an especially gifted human, if we had someone like that, probably couldn't safely navigate the universe now."

General Jackson peered at Doctor Lewellen with the expression of someone hiding a secret but wanting to disclose it.

"What?" the doctor asked.

"I haven't told you everything," General Jackson said. "Not all of the astronauts declined."

Doctor Lewellen's eyes widened.

"Captain Trace called me this morning. Said she had thought about the mission a lot and was willing to volunteer for the sake of mankind, but she wasn't willing to throw her life away on a mission that couldn't succeed."

"What do you mean?"

"She will go, if we can guarantee success probability of greater than 50 percent." He searched the scientist's face. "Can we honestly say that?"

Doctor Lewellen shook his head before it fell.

CHAPTER 8

NGC 4880 lay 1,001,459 light years beyond the Sombrero Galaxy. The ultra-compact galaxy was only two hundred light years across and home to about one hundred million stars. It was tiny compared to the Milky Way, which was one hundred thousand light years in diameter and contained two hundred billion stars. However, the condensed nature of NGC 4880 made it special among inhabited places in the universe. Intelligent civilizations in various star systems found it practical to reach one another within NGC 4880, allowing for collaboration and cooperation concerning areas of scientific and technological achievement. The result was an entire galaxy of advanced beings making scientific advancements together. Though there were many different languages, they adopted a means of universal communication through a nano-computer known as the raditron. Travel faster than light speed was achieved through the transformation of matter into photons that were energized by electromagnetic bundle enhancement, a sort of light slingshot technology. The inhabitants of NGC 4880 had protected themselves from the ravages of intruding asteroids, meteors, gamma ray bursts, charged particle eruptions, and cosmic rays by enveloping each of their worlds in a force field created by aggregating helium atoms into an impenetrable, invisible latticework fed by atom projectors on the planets' surfaces. Limitless energy was enjoyed from cold fusion reactions that produced no nuclear waste.

Yet, the most remarkable achievement of these beings was their system of governance. All inhabitants of this galaxy communicated by way of brain wave plangency, whereby their thoughts were captured, organized, enhanced, and shared instantly through plane waves captured and transmitted by the raditrons implanted in their brains at birth. There was no need for external computers or a dizzying conglomeration of software. Thought was transformed instantly to communication between all beings in NGC 4880. Thus, they governed by way of majority rule on a grass roots level across the galaxy without need of representatives or political leaders or the corruption and self-aggrandizement outside worlds had experienced with other forms of governance. So effective was their system that the collective morality had eliminated crime, poverty, disease, and inequality. Inhabitants lived to an average age of one thousand years.

Life had evolved into a blissful existence dominated by higher pursuits such as art, music, intellectual discussion, scientific enlightenment, exploration of the universe, and pleasant personal association.

A day, however, came when bliss turned into concern, followed by terror. The phase transition had ignited and was rushing toward NGC 4880. Due to its close proximity, the cosmic calamity would reach their galaxy in a matter of weeks after it had erupted at the edge of the universe.

Scientific discussion morphed into heated debate. What was the best course for survival—escape, protection, or attack? Some of the scientists argued for mass teleportation to distant worlds. However, that proposal was not practical since there were no receiving devices outside of NGC 4880 and too little time to install them. Perhaps a fusion bomb would stop the transition. That suggestion was also not workable since there were no weapons in the galaxy. None had been needed in more than a million years. And then it became clear to them. The solution was in the atom shields that protected their worlds so completely from outside threats. Preparations were taken to enhance each shield to ensure maximum effect.

As the inhabitants of NGC 4880 watched the fire grow closer, their shields deflected intense radiation, swarms of rocky rubble from crushed planets and moons, powerful gravitational waves, withering heat, and blinding photons.

The transition reached NGC 4880 more rapidly than their scientists had predicted, but their force fields were in place. Perhaps they would hold as the menace passed them by.

Collective thinking became a nightmarish amalgam of fear, anger, hope, wonder, and scientific interest in the fire that enveloped their galaxy. "How long would the force fields hold? What would be the nature of this new universe? How would their galaxy exist in a universe of different physical laws? Could they survive as an island within transformed matter and energy? Would life return to normal? How could such advanced beings let this happen? Should they have seen the disaster coming long ago and taken steps to survive when there was no crisis? Who was to blame for this catastrophe?"

Every soul of NGC 4880 had watched the blinding fire approach, turning stars and planets into dark areas of a changed universe filled with bizarre atoms not yet amalgamated into new cosmic bodies. All too soon, it enveloped NGC 4880 in intense electromagnetic energy the inhabitants regarded with trembling and fascination. It moved past at enormous speed on a path of destruction, and they breathed a collective sigh of relief, believing their force fields had deflected the heat and radiation that had destroyed other worlds. Then the cosmos outside of their protective bubbles began to twinkle. Something in the new universe was reacting with their force fields. A strange electrical interaction was doing deadly work. Once impenetrable, the force fields began to evaporate as helium atoms changed into a new form of matter. Deadly twinkling reactions moved downward toward the planets of NGC 4880. To their horror, the inhabitants observed mountains, land masses, seas, rivers, and structures disappear. Atmospheres thinned, and breathing labored before it stopped. Mortal bodies disintegrated. Frantic attempts to seek refuge underground or to escape in spacecraft were futile. NGC 4880 and the space-time in which it had existed were no more.

CHAPTER 9

Doctor Jessup sat quietly at the back of the classroom and watched Bobby Alderson do a problem in integral calculus. He barely managed to control his pride. "You go, Bobby. Show them how smart you are," he said under his breath.

The students then broke into groups of two for the calculus rumble, a test of mathematics ability done in rapid-fire fashion where teams face off. The loser sits and is replaced by another team, until only the champion remains.

Bobby and Clarissa Newhall, a deceptively shy student with the heart of a wolverine, faced two students who taunted them—football stars with high IQs but little else.

The teacher placed a picture on the overhead projector and asked, "What is the length of this arc?"

One of the football stars hit his bell and recited an answer, only to be shot down by an annoying buzzer.

"The question goes to you," the teacher said as she pointed to Bobby and Clarissa.

Bobby smiled and recited the correct answer. Most of the students cheered and clapped, but the football players and their team cohorts made goofy faces followed by derisive glares directed at Bobby's team.

And so it went, until Bobby and Clarissa stood as the champions to the applause and words of support from their admirers: "Way to go, Bobby. Great job, Clarissa. You're the champs! Smartest kids in the school."

Clarissa gave that wry smile that said, "I kicked your butt, sucker," while Bobby beamed, blushed, and turned away as if to say, "No big thing." But it really was.

Class ended, and the students filed from the room chattering about things of teen importance.

One of the vanquished football players raised his voice in schadenfreude. "Yeah, retard bozos may be able to read and learn to recite, like a parrot, but they could never play a skill position. Glad I'm not a Downs freak." He used both fingers to lift the outer corners of his eyelids. "You Chinese?" he said with a laugh.

Other football players whistled and laughed. The two athlete game partners gave each other high fives.

Miss Saunders, the math teacher, glared at the offenders before turning to Bobby. "I'm so sorry. That was rude and completely wrong. You are a smart guy, and I'm very proud of you."

"It's okay. He didn't mean it. Probably isn't used to losing. Not his fault. He's good at a lot of stuff."

She blinked at the response. "Oh Bobby, you are a special person," Miss Saunders said with a motherly hug.

Bobby shuffled off with a fellow student offering effusive praise.

Doctor Jessup approached Miss Saunders from the audience. "How is Bobby doing in math? I got here a little while ago and really enjoyed the competition. He seemed terrific at it."

"Doctor, glad to see you. Sorry for the bad behavior. That student's father is on the school board and he's popular. That's makes it difficult to stop his insolent conduct. But, our zero tolerance policy has helped us stop most of the aggressive bullying. That's some progress." Miss Saunders refocused. "Bobby's math work? Great. As on every test. He did so well today in class, amazing really. Are you still monitoring him?"

"Yes. That will go on for his entire life. Funny thing about his intellect. We just administered a new IQ test, and he seems to be getting smarter. I wouldn't have thought it possible. Before Bobby, that is."

"Why is that happening?" she asked.

"Most likely because his brain began to develop very fast when we deactivated the defective genetic material. Normal brains start to develop at birth. Bobby's brain began that process much later, and it seems to be trying to catch up as a way of compensating for lost time, but as a mature organ. He is progressing at an accelerated rate."

"That correlates with our spatial calculus game," she said.

"How does that work?" Doctor Jessup glanced around the room searching for the answer, as though printed on a poster.

"It's an IQ test of a specific math skill in video game format. The student sits before a screen and is presented with space travel problems. They can be solved only by the application of spatial calculus, but without the use of a calculator. The student uses mental computations that must be done fast and correctly to avoid the asteroid or black hole or radiation burst. Eye-hand coordination is involved but plays a minor role to score points. Mental ability is the main tool. Quick, correct thinking is what really raises the student's score. Kind of like riding a mountain bike down unmarked terrain around rocks and trees by figuring out maneuvers beforehand."

Doctor Jessup massaged his chin as though he had a goatee. "You don't say. How has Bobby done as compared with the other students?"

Her eyes brightened. "Remarkably well. He scores perfect almost every run. No other student has done that, not even our most gifted pupils. Now, don't get me wrong. Some of them have tested very well, too, but not at the same level as Bobby. He is alone at the top. Bobby's average score correlates to an IQ of about . . . Let me see."

She retrieved a booklet from her desk, scanned a page, and said, "Well, at least in spatial calculus it would be somewhere around one hundred ninety-six."

Doctor Jessup suddenly was lost in deep thought. He became silent and unresponsive to her, until he realized the situation and said, "Please forgive me. I need to think about the implications of what you just said."

He turned, head down, eyes focused on the floor, mind somewhere else, and walked from the school.

Doctor Jessup's phone rang. He glanced at it blankly, still in deep reflection, not focusing on the caller ID information. Then he thought about his wife and answered.

A familiar voice said, "Jessup. I have an emergency meeting in Houston this week. Heavy stuff. Sure would like to lighten things a bit with another dinner and some pleasant reminiscing. Got time, say Friday?"

"Sure thing, Ayana. I have some pretty thought-provoking things going on here. About that genetic engineering program we discussed last visit. You might find it interesting. Seems to now involve advanced math capability. Right up your alley."

"Intriguing. Be there Friday. Pick me up at the same place and time?"

"Sounds good. Looking forward to it."

"Doctor Ayana, do you still calculate that the heavy element may stop the transition? Keep in mind that it was delivered but had no effect," General Jackson said in the high-level scientific meeting at the Johnson Space Center.

"The element should work. It was not the problem. As I warned, the probe must be delivered to a precise point to reverse the transition. All the data seem to suggest that such precision was not achieved. If my work is right about the nature of the transition, our heavy element can reverse it by changing the transitioned matter back to its previous state."

"I hope that's right because the president has authorized another mission, this time using a seasoned astronaut who has volunteered. Our best man." General Jackson's jaw was set.

Doctor Ayana said, "Radiation was more intense than anticipated. Seems unlikely any human could do better in that environment."

Doctor Lewellen held up a photo of stars. "Just got this from Whiteside. Yesterday, he observed even more dangerous conditions than before due to the transition getting closer. His instruments detected stronger gravitational waves and more intense radiation. These stars are out of place."

"Our astronaut is willing to try. Maybe better shielding will provide just enough time to hit the target." General Jackson took a deep breath. "It's the only chance we have."

Doctor Lewellen's forehead wrinkled. "I thought all the astronauts had declined. Who is this volunteer?"

"Colonel Archie Rhorbach," General Jackson answered.

"Rhorbach. First man to set foot on Mars. He must be at least seventy-five." Doctor Lewellen's contorted face evidenced disapprobation, if not disbelief.

General Jackson became defensive. "Seventy-eight, to be exact. I can tell you that he's in great shape. Runs marathons. Trains our astronauts. Has more space flight experience than anyone else. That's only part of the reason he volunteered, though. Rhorbach says he has lived his life and isn't afraid to sacrifice for humanity. His wife is gone, and he has no children. No one to leave behind. Besides, he believes space is his destiny. A sort of final resting place as a tribute to his career."

The room became silent as the scientists and officials considered the news: an elderly astronaut going on a one-way mission that younger astronauts had eschewed, one requiring extraordinary stamina and ability that a shielded quantum computer did not possess, to deliver a payload at a precise point in the vastness of the cosmos, despite intense radiation and dislodged asteroids flying at him like machine gun bullets, to save the universe. What were the odds he would succeed?

Bobby Alderson played peek-a-boo with the baby, trying to make him coo, smile, respond, anything to break out of his autistic prison. He tried again, and again, seemingly with endless patience.

"Why you doin' that? Just a waste of time if you ask me. Ain't nothin' in his head. He's retarded," attendant Anthony said.

"That's not true, Mr. Anthony. He's autistic. That can be helped with a lot of work. Takes time." Bobby smiled in his usual friendly way.

Anthony hissed. "You don't tell me about dumb kids, Mr. Know-It-All. I been doin' this for eleven years, and I've learned a thing or two about the residents here."

"Sorry, sir. You are right. I shouldn't tell you your work. But, can I still try to help a little? It'll save you looking after him for a while."

Anthony scoffed. "Suit yourself."

"Bobby, the bus is here for school. I'll take care of Jonathan," nurse Angie Tolston said.

Bobby made one more coo. "Miss Angie, look. I think he smiled a little bit."

"All right, students. Today we play the spatial calculus game again, but this time against Norman, a remote super computer that holds the high score of 149,589,610. We will use multiple stations to speed up the process and see how everyone stacks up against Norman's artificial brain." Miss Saunders seemed as excited as some of the students. "Get ready. We'll go randomly by groups of five. Form a line."

The first students took positions at their computer terminals, and the game was on. Spaceships encountered black hole event horizons, intense magnetar fields, pulsar sweeps of deadly electromagnetic energy, speeding asteroids, comet tails of dust and gas, neutron star mergers producing intense gamma ray and X-ray bursts, and gravitational waves that flung planets and moons into space. Vectors, angles, curves, distances, velocities, deviations, and other navigational problems needed immediate calculation for the pilots to avoid terminal cosmic dangers. One misstep meant virtual disaster and the end of point accretion.

One by one they went down, some accumulating record scores for humans, but Norman stood alone. There was one last group to play, and it included Bobby Alderson. The students sat at their terminals. Some adjusted seats, while others did finger exercises before clutching their joysticks.

Bobby ignored those inanities but, instead, looked at his cell phone, on which he activated the music app. He selected a certain song, and it came to life, "Hero Rider":

> *Ridin' across the clouds,*
> *Around them rocks in sight;*
> *Comin' for my sweetie;*
> *Have some faith tonight;*
> *Over towerin' waves,*
> *I'm screamin' for the shore,*
> *Ridin' to you at first light,*
> *The gal who I adore.*

One of the brainy football players rolled his eyes, but Bobby paid no attention to him, preferring to focus on the monitor, which suddenly shone with a dizzying array of speeding objects, energy bursts, particle swarms, ominous black wells, and multiple-lined waves.

Bobby's song played on, and he responded to it with the intense focus of a big cat that was after some prey and the deft ability to snatch it.

"Shit," "damn," "crap," and silence came from the other players as each of their screens froze with scores ranging from 68,876,900 to

111,843,132, but Bobby kept going, riding space-time through the cosmos, avoiding visible dangers, hugging the safe peripheries of energy blasts, and navigating around swallowing darkness. His score soared: 99,336,021; 112,223,988; 136,436,011; 155,148,573; and, finally, 200,000,101. The computer monitor went blank for a moment before it flashed a message: "Congratulations, you have successfully crossed the universe. You beat Norman."

Most of Bobby's classmates went wild. "Man, you whupped up on Norman." "Incredible!" "Way to go." "Vegas here we come." "Smart dude." Some whistled and clapped; others patted him on the back.

One of the football players snorted and pushed through the others. He angrily said, "Your stupid music."

Bobby blinked.

The football player got close to Bobby's face. "It distracted me. I could have done better. You made me screw up. I ought to bust up your phone."

"Sorry. It makes me go like a zippy rabbit," Bobby said with a smile.

"Zippy rabbit," the football player hissed. "I'll zip your rabbit."

Miss Saunders came between them. "Stop it. Class is over. I'll have no bullying." She stared down the football player. "I can go to the principal right now if that's what you want. Remember our zero-tolerance policy against bullying. That would keep you from playing sports."

"Whatever," the football player said sarcastically. "But he has no business in this class. It's not for morons on drugs." He walked away with his teammates.

She placed a reassuring hand on Bobby's shoulder. "You just defeated a super computer. Nobody has ever beaten it before now. Did you know the game is a learning program? Gets tougher the better you do. Figures out your strengths and makes the problems harder. That's great. Unbelievable, really."

"It's just math," he said with a child-like smile. "No biggie. It's not savin' somebody's life or important stuff like that."

"Just math?" Miss Saunders started laughing, and soon Bobby was laughing with her.

"Doctor Jessup. Hi, this is Miss Saunders."

He responded with a pleasant greeting.

"That's right. We met before at the high school. I just wanted to call and tell you something incredible. Today Bobby beat Norman, a super computer, on the calculus space game."

She listened and said, "No, this is the first time we competed against the computer. In the past our students played each other. My understanding is that no other high school student in the country has defeated Norman. Bobby is the first and only one. I think you ought to test his IQ again. My reference book doesn't cover his level of intellect."

Doctor Jessup's excited voice came from the speaker.

"I totally agree," she said. "He is a special person with unique talents. Who knows? Maybe, in the future, he will discover a cure for some terrible disease or reverse dementia or even be the first person to travel to another star system."

CHAPTER **10**

Doctor Jessup looked fondly at a picture of Bobby on his desk. "We did it, you and I. What incredible things will you do? I can only imagine."

He leaned back, closed his eyes, and relaxed in contemplation. No possibility seemed beyond his ken. Soon, he was napping. Doctor Jessup's mind raced backward and forward in time between historical achievements and future hopes, causing a rollercoaster of emotions. As deep sleep took hold, dreams came forth.

"Mrs. James, this is Doctor Jessup. We just received FDA approval. I would like to talk with you about our subject. Would you have time today?" He was excited, almost giddy, an unusual emotion for a scientist.

He listened and responded, "Great. I'll be there at three. I'm looking forward to meeting Bobby."

That afternoon, he was sitting in the office of Pricilla James, the director of Bright Lighthouse. She was a no-nonsense, sixty-year-old woman who had devoted her career to caring for special-needs people.

Her intense eyes and smileless face foreshadowed the woman's dutiful strength and resolve.

She wasted no time in her discussion with Doctor Jessup. "Congratulations on receiving government approval for your genetics engineering treatment. However, I, as guardian for our orphaned residents, must give my permission. Do you understand?"

"Absolutely. That is a condition of the approval."

"I am not convinced this is a good thing for Bobby or anyone else. Our residents are human beings, not guinea pigs. There won't be any experimentation on them. I will need to be convinced your drug is in their best interest. You must accept the challenge of proving that to me before we go any further in this matter."

"I understand and agree. However, this is not experimentation. We did that with mice over the past three years by targeting a gene that produces neurological defects in rodents. This series of injections is the first of our human trials. If we are successful, a wonderful change will occur in Bobby."

"And if you are not?" she asked sternly.

"In that event, and I believe it is unlikely, the person will not be any worse off than before. Our drug targets a specific gene, the one that causes Down syndrome. No others. I am convinced it is safe."

"Doctor Jessup, do you know why I am even considering this project for one of our residents?"

"I don't know exactly why. Probably because you want to help a person with Downs."

"Yes, surely that, but also because of your character. I checked you out, and my sources said you are not only a brilliant scientist but that you also are a good man who cares about helping disadvantaged people, as I do." She stared askance at him. "This is not about your receiving some scientific award, is it?"

"Absolutely not. I would like to provide relief for those who are suffering, especially people born with genetic defects." He removed his glasses, rubbed tired eyes, and said, "I am convinced we can help some of them live better lives. And, who knows, maybe in time they will return the favor by helping others. I have the feeling there are many special minds waiting to be released." He pointed toward a picture of a Downs child on her desk.

She seemed lost considering something ethereal. "I have tried for years to provide the best care possible for special-needs persons. The reality, however, is that I find it increasingly difficult to hire employees who share my compassion. Oh, most are sincere at first, but they lose patience over time. It's not easy handling the duties here. After a while, many times I detect some degree of abuse or neglect in certain employees and must terminate them, and the cycle begins again." Mrs. James made eye contact. "If you can truly reverse Downs and free some of our residents to live normally in society, then they will no longer need institutional care. I pray you can do that for them."

"I pray for that, too."

She pushed up from her chair and looked down at him. "Come with me."

They walked a short distance until she stopped inside the doorway to a large room with special-needs wards. Some watched television; others played with toys and stuffed animals; and two sat alone rocking back and forth.

"This is rest time. We bring in our residents from the yard, where we try and let them get some exercise and fresh air. The attendants are always with them." She gestured toward white-uniformed people in the room.

He asked, "Those seated over there, the ones doing the rocking. Are they afflicted with Downs?"

"Yes, and autism as well. They are imprisoned in their own worlds, and we cannot reach them. There is no meaningful response to human contact. We provide palliative and protective care. Unfortunately, that is all we can do."

"A pity. Maybe someday we can find a cure for them," he responded.

She smiled for the first time Doctor Jessup could remember. "I am glad you are so confident. Let's go see Bobby."

Mrs. James led him to a group of residents playing with various toys and wooden puzzles. They giggled and laughed without any apparent care for whether or not the large puzzle pieces or building blocks fit together correctly.

Mrs. James kneeled and spoke gently. "Bobby?"

A young man with oriental features and a short, rotund body looked up at her. "Yes, ma'am."

"There is someone here to see you. Would you like to meet him?"

"Oh yeah. I like nice people." He stood, leaving colorful plastic blocks in disarray.

The scientist extended a hand. "Bobby, I am Doctor Jessup. Glad to be here with you."

Bobby's eyes glistened. He clutched Doctor Jessup's hand with both of his. "Did you come to adopt me? That has been my dream. I'd like going to a real family. Did you?" He seemed to search Doctor Jessup's face for an answer.

"I, I . . ." A lump began to form in Doctor's Jessup's throat. His eyes felt moist. He found it difficult to tell the truth of his visit and shatter this vulnerable child's dream. Finally, he mustered the courage and strength to say, "Bobby, I am here to be kind of like a father, I guess, and to do good for you, just like a father does with his son."

"Wow. A father, for me? Thank you, thank you, thank you." He gripped Doctor Jessup's hand harder.

Mrs. James raised an eyebrow.

Doctor Jessup kneeled to be at eye level with Bobby. "Tell you what. I will come every week and we can play games and talk and even take a ride in my car. Would you like that?"

"Oh, yes, yes, yes. I like rides in cars. Can we get some ice cream?"

Doctor Jessup glanced at Mrs. James.

She nodded.

Doctor Jessup felt more reassured. "You bet. Ice cream it will be. Bobby, there is something else I need to tell you."

Bobby's sanguine expression seemed to say, "Sure. I trust you." It softened Doctor Jessup's resolve to explain more.

Then he found the emotional strength to continue. "I will need to give you a shot, just one, each week when I visit."

Bobby's facial expression quickly changed. "What for? I don't like shots. They hurt. Is it a big needle?"

"To make you well from your Downs. So you can be like other kids. Go to school, maybe even college." He stopped, only to remember something more. "And the needle is real small. You won't hardly feel it."

Bobby looked at Mrs. James, other residents, and the colorful blocks, before returning his attention to Doctor Jessup. "Will you give me the shot? I won't be scared if you will be the person to do it."

"No one else, Bobby. Only me."

"Then, okay." Bobby was smiling widely again. "I know my new father won't hurt me."

Over the course of the next six weeks Doctor Jessup came to Bright Lighthouse. Each week he administered the drug he hoped would deactivate the Down syndrome gene. He also took Bobby on rides for ice cream to fulfill his promise to the boy. During these visits he played games with Bobby to determine whether his intellectual ability was changing. To his dismay, Bobby's learning capacity remained the same at the sixth week. Doctor Jessup began to lose faith that his work could reverse Down syndrome. He carefully reviewed his research in an effort to detect where he had gone wrong.

While reading through his notes, Doctor Jessup's phone rang.

He mumbled to himself. "Not now, please. This is not a good time." He was not in an upbeat mood.

The caller left no message and tried again.

He threw the papers on his desk and answered bruskly. "What is it?"

"Doctor Jessup, this is Mrs. James. I have some information you will want to know."

"Oh, please excuse me, Mrs. James. I didn't realize it was you." He felt ashamed at his rude behavior. "I was wrestling with a problem. Please forgive me. How may I help you?"

"It's Bobby. I believe you should come over here as soon as you can."

A coldness swept through him. Maybe the drug had produced some unwanted side effect, perhaps something harmful. "Is he all right? Bobby isn't sick, I hope."

"No, thankfully nothing like that," she answered.

"What then?"

"Come and see for yourself. Better that you observe in person than talking about it over the phone. Can you visit us today?"

"Sure. Now you have got me interested and scared at the same time. I'll be right there," he said.

"You have me really worried," Doctor Jessup said breathlessly as he and Mrs. James hurried down the hallway toward the activities room in Bright Lighthouse.

They arrived, and Bobby looked at Doctor Jessup from something that had held his attention. He jumped from the floor and ran to the scientist with papers tightly gripped in one hand.

Bobby offered the papers. "Here, these are for you. A gift. For my new father. Do you like them?"

Doctor Jessup laughed and said, "Thank you. What are they?" He unfolded the papers, examined the content, and studied Bobby. "Who did this work?"

Bobby beamed, his cheeks as full as those of a squirrel holding nuts. "I did, all by myself."

"You? But, this is algebra. How did you learn it?"

"From a math video Mrs. James gave me yesterday. I watched the whole thing. It's fun. Starting to do geometry now. I like it even better. Shapes are interesting and cool. Do you like shapes?" His eyes were bright with questions.

Doctor Jessup was thunderstruck for a few moments, until he said to Mrs. James, "How could he do this math so quickly?"

She tried to speak but her voice broke. Several deep breaths allowed her to say, "Your drug, Doctor. It worked. The miracle I doubted. But you were right. How wonderful for Bobby. He wants to go to school with the normal children. His enthusiasm is marvelous."

Bobby returned his attention to unsolved mathematics challenges. He hummed as his unleashed mind flew through a new geometry problem.

CHAPTER **11**

Deep sleep would not come for Bobby. He tossed and turned in a state of crepuscular light from nagging worries about starting middle school the next day. His mind and heart had combined to force fearful thoughts on the teenager: What would the other students think of him? Could he really do the schoolwork they did? Would mean kids make fun of his appearance? And the bullies he had heard about, would they hurt him? Maybe he should just stay at Bright Lighthouse where he felt safe.

Through the dark mentations a light appeared, distant and dim, but a point of hope, nonetheless. Bobby watched the light grow closer in his mind's eye. His unconscious percipience was as clear as a conscious sense impression. The light became a yellow star. He experienced the star coming closer, until Bobby's mind grasped that he was traveling toward it.

Bobby felt warmth from the star. His mental anguish began to wane, driven from him much the same as a fire replaces the chill of a winter night. Yet, it was not temperature that was changing his thoughts and feelings but, rather, the energy from his mind searching for answers to mysteries he yearned to solve.

A simulacrum of the cosmos spread out before him.

He moved faster and faster, not past the roiling ball of gas, but through its glowing atmosphere into the fission core. Atoms of hydrogen became evident. He observed bursts of gamma rays from the atoms smashing together to form helium atoms. Gamma rays struggled toward the surface, being absorbed and ejected from densely packed atoms along the way until, after what he understood to be thousands of years had passed, they burst from the star as visible light.

Soon the star was behind Bobby as he continued into deep space. The cratered surface of Mercury evidenced bright crater rays. Bobby could sense the planet's eight-hundred-degree Fahrenheit sunlit areas. A cloud-shrouded planet came into view, and Bobby's journey took him into its heavy atmosphere, one hundred sixty miles to Venus's rocky surface. He could feel the atmosphere's immense pressure, scorching temperatures reaching four hundred fifty degrees Celsius, and tornadic winds exceeding two hundred miles per hour.

A pleasingly blue planet appeared next, the earth, his home. He yearned to stop and feel warm breezes, smell pine trees and roses, hear children laughing, savor a tasty treat; yet, Bobby went on, past the planet he knew. The youth became aware that his mind was in control of a journey to understand wonders not yet familiar to him.

The rusty surface of Mars loomed ahead. Bobby swooped down and slowed across the rocky, cold, dry terrain of this alien world. He dipped into a massive crater formed by a meteorite impact billions of years ago, then sped northward to the Martian pole where water ice was thick and vast.

Through the rocky remnants of a planet that never formed, known as the asteroid belt, Bobby flew until massive Jupiter dominated his view of space. Bands of multi-colored gas covered the planet, punctuated by a red whirlwind larger than the earth. He could feel the force of this gas giant's massive gravity that had created the asteroid belt by preventing matter from aggregating into a planet at the dawn of the solar system four and a half billion years ago.

Saturn's bright, icy rings reflected sunlight. Bobby shot into the rings of dust, sand grains, pebbles, and rocks covered in water ice. He penetrated Saturn's thick atmosphere of hydrogen, helium, methane, and ammonia, finally reaching a rocky core of extreme heat and atmospheric pressure.

At light speed he headed toward the outer vapor worlds Uranus and Neptune. Bobby enjoyed the light blue atmosphere of Uranus and noticed that the planet rotated from bottom to top due to its axis being parallel to the plane of the solar system rather than perpendicular to it. Neptune's dark blue atmosphere evidenced violent weather phenomena driven by the fastest winds recorded among the sun's planets.

Pluto followed, a rocky body demoted to planetoid status because of its diminutive size.

Bobby proceeded into deep space, trillions of miles from the sun. The Kuiper Belt's disk-like conglomeration of asteroids and comets stretched as far as he could see, but Bobby's speed soon took him through to another region of space.

A bubble of loose rocks infused with water ice swirled lazily around the solar system. The Ort Cloud was home to billions of comets waiting to be dislodged from their weak orbits. Bobby's mind saw this cosmic engine at work. A frozen mountain was sent hurtling toward the sun by gravity from an invisible body, perhaps the fabled "Ninth Planet," yet to be discovered but theorized by scientists. His mental senses searched for the elusive body but saw only the darkness of empty space, until, there it was, not a planet but a black hole lurking in a region of space beyond the sun's solar wind, the heliopause. The gravity monster was waiting to devour matter and energy that could not escape a singularity in space smaller than an atom.

Bobby awoke from his cosmic dream-adventure. "Man, school's gonna be so much fun now that I have this good brain. Can't wait."

Bobby's excitement faded into weariness. He closed his eyes and drifted into restful sleep.

CHAPTER 12

"Jessup, I need to tell you something important." Doctor Ayana lost himself for a moment in the bottom of his Manhattan. Candlelight flickered off the crystal glass. He sighed, as though cleansing his lungs of some foul air. Finally, he raised his eyes to stare directly at those of Doctor Jessup. "I am going to disclose a matter to you. It's classified. But, at this point, what the hell? Doesn't really matter now I suppose."

"What in the world are you talking about, Ayana? Classified stuff. Doesn't matter. Sounds very dramatic," Doctor Jessup said.

Doctor Ayana got close to his ear. "We are in the midst of a catastrophe." He paused to glance around. "Jessup, there is a cosmic phenomenon approaching. It is a kind of physical transformation from our matter to something completely different. Called a phase transition. Consuming our universe as it approaches, atom by atom."

Doctor Jessup swallowed. He tried to speak but stopped to find the right words. Finally, he blurted out, "Are you being serious, Ayana? Consuming the entire universe. How can that be? I've never heard of such a thing. Well, maybe in theory, but not as a practical threat, except for a black hole, which couldn't destroy everything."

"I assure you the phase transition is real. Cosmologists have theorized that the atomic structure of our universe could change into a new form of matter, one with different properties and physical laws. The transition began far from the Milky Way. It is coming toward us and will destroy everything it touches. We have confirmed this is happening now from our deep space instruments."

Doctor Jessup guzzled his drink to cool a sensation of heat rising in his stomach. "My God. Can we stop it? Perhaps with a nuclear weapon, or maybe a fleet of them."

Doctor Ayana said, "We launched a robotic probe to deliver a new element that could reverse the transition, but it failed. Probably due to intense radiation in that region of space. Or maybe our computer just missed the target. Who knows for sure?"

"And that's it? We won't send a second probe to try. What about a manned craft?"

Ayana whispered. "It's a suicide mission. No human can survive the radiation. All of the current astronauts declined. Recently, however, a retired astronaut volunteered. He said he's willing to die in space. Older guy, but seemed able."

Doctor Jessup waited in silence for more information, as Doctor Ayana peered across the dimly lit room, apparently to gather his thoughts. He shook his head. "Horrible luck, though. The worst possible thing happened. I got word this afternoon. That retired astronaut, the one who volunteered, he had a heart attack. Survived but is in intensive care."

"And the mission?"

"There will be none. It would be futile to send another unmanned craft. And a piloted mission probably wouldn't be successful either. Even a highly trained astronaut would need enhanced skill to have any realistic chance of success, and there is no one, even in the military, like that." Doctor Ayana downed his drink and motioned to the waiter. "Another. Make it a double."

"No one, you say." Doctor Jessup focused intensely on his friend for a moment before his eyes stared off in the distance as thoughts and emotions arose in his mind and heart. Surprise, fear, anger, determination to find an answer, and, finally, acceptance tore through the man. Then an endearing notion took hold, perhaps from mental exhaustion or, more likely, as a defensive mechanism to turn from something painful to someone who made him happy—Bobby. "You mentioned special skills. That's an interesting subject to me these days. Exactly what talents would you like to see in a person?"

Doctor Ayana looked at him with a blank stare. "Talents?" His mind obviously had jumped to another subject.

"The special skills or talents or qualities you think an astronaut would need to do this mission. Like you just told me. It's an engrossing discussion because of my work. I have my own idea about ideal qualities in a person. You?" Doctor Jessup was smiling, just a bit, as though the involuntary defensive psychological mechanism was working.

"Yes, of course. Well, he, or she, should have almost superhuman ability to pilot the spacecraft through a flurry of radiation bursts, gravitational and magnetic influences, and planetary rubble from cosmic collisions caused by distortions of space-time. It would be like navigating a ship through powerful currents and waves of a winter gale, around icebergs and rocky islands. Very difficult, even for an experienced helmsman. Our ideal pilot would need quickly to compensate for cosmic anomalies to maintain course and avoid being thrown into space, possibly to be gobbled up by a black hole or incinerated by a star. A computer alone was able to do the mission when we first detected the phase transition. At that time the universe wasn't as corrupted as it is now. But today, I doubt a computer alone would be able to fly to the transition and hit the target. Not intuitive enough to handle the fast-moving distortions, and no proven data to load into the computer's memory for reliable AI operations. The mission really requires a human with exceptional skill to guide the craft to the right point in space and deliver our element to a target that won't even be revealed until the last second." He sneered. "We probably need the best video game player in the world."

Doctor Jessup held up a hand to the waiter. "A double for me, too." He turned his full attention to Doctor Ayana. "You mean one of the smartest people in the world, who is flawless at video games, and is a whiz in applied math, like spatial calculus, and who can compute in his head better than a computer, fast and accurately, who is healthy enough to fly into deep space, and is so altruistic as to volunteer for a hopeless mission. I like to think humans can be that way and we will always have the upper hand over machines. After all, I've dedicated my life to human enhancement."

Doctor Ayana blinked at his friend's informational effusion. He lifted his glass slowly, sipped his drink, and exhaled deeply. "Yes, that would be the perfect candidate. But there is no one like that, at least as far as I know."

The waiter placed Doctor Jessup's drink before him. He studied the liquid gold for several seconds. His smile broadened slightly. "You know that boy I introduced you to, the one with Downs? Your description reminds me somewhat of him." The smile persisted. "Of course, he's just a kid, but I'm really proud of him. And, I guess, a bit protective, too." The smile faded. "This catastrophe you mentioned has me worried about him. That it will cut short his promising life before he has a chance to live as a normal person. I hope it doesn't happen. Bobby is such a good boy. Has overcome a lot. He's so happy we reversed his birth defect, which has allowed his brain to perform at an elevated level. Loves school. He seems to be learning at an accelerated pace. Much faster than someone with normal intelligence. He's way ahead of the other kids, even the gifted ones. What a boy. Well, he isn't really a boy anymore, I suppose, since he's eighteen, and he finished his high school courses early. Just taking advanced subjects for fun, calculus and physics. He wants to graduate with his class next month. Has a bright future, really a good life ahead. I can't even imagine him losing that chance to something from space that could kill everyone, not to mention all of the other people with genetic defects who now can be helped by our work."

"Yes, Bobby, at Bright Lighthouse," Doctor Ayana responded with obvious interest. "How could I forget him?"

"That's correct." Doctor Jessup swished his drink while thinking, and then said, "He just tested perfect on a spatial calculus video game. His teacher told me he's the only student to score that high, even among the bright kids. He beat a super computer called Norman. No one else has done that. It seems the computer doesn't like to lose. Keeps ramping up the level of difficulty as the game progresses." He chuckled. "But that didn't stop Bobby. He navigated a virtual spacecraft across the cosmos by computing a course in his head to avoid dangers like asteroids, gamma rays, and black holes. His mind works real fast and accurately. He solves advanced math problems in his head. And you talk about altruism." Doctor Jessup murmured. "The only person I know who truly cares about others. Forgives bullies. Some loving quality from his Downs genetics remains. Thank God."

Doctor Jessup looked up from his pleasant thoughts about Bobby and was struck by Doctor Ayana's demeanor. The mathematician was staring at him with the intense eyes of a predator.

CHAPTER 13

"Doctor Jessup, please. You have got to help him." The woman's voice was almost panicked.

"Who is this?"

"Miss Saunders, Bobby's teacher from high school," blurted from the cell phone. "We met a while ago. I've called you about his academic progress. You must remember me."

"Yes, of course. What is the problem?"

"It's Bobby. They came and took him away. I tried to stop them, but they said it was a matter of national security. You are the only person I can think of to call about this."

"What people are you talking about?"

"Government agents. From the FBI probably. I really don't know for sure. But one thing was especially strange."

"What's that?"

"They were led by a very tall black man. He had an accent and said he worked for NASA. Why would NASA be interested in Bobby? He isn't involved with the government."

"I'll take care of it." Doctor Jessup dialed a number on his phone. A man answered.

"Ayana, did you come for Bobby Alderson?"

"I'm sorry, Jessup. I couldn't tell you. They wouldn't let me. Classified stuff. I mentioned it the last time we visited."

"Damn it, Ayana, I spoke to you in confidence. As friends. My comments about Bobby were strictly a matter of personal interest. And maybe some pride for what we had achieved. I was not offering up my patient for your suicide space mission. He's just a kid."

"You said he was eighteen, an adult under the law. And he came of his own free will. I explained that we had a special need he might be able to assist us with and asked for his help. He agreed. And, Jessup, he is smart, just as you said, really smart. Hell, he did math problems for us, and in some areas he's better than me. What a mind."

"That's right, he is damn smart, and you had nothing to do with it. Besides, he has no maturity. Bobby can't make life-and-death decisions. Emotionally he is undeveloped. You are taking advantage of an impressionable youth, an innocent Pollyanna."

"Jessup, I have an obligation to the world. There is only a single chance to save humanity. One person, whether you or me or even someone else, can't stand in the way of this mission. It's too important for billions of people."

"Where is he? At least tell me that so I can go to him. I want to comfort Bobby. He is an orphan and thinks of me as his father. I need to know where he is."

Doctor Ayana hesitated but relented. "All right. He's at Johnson. In the administrative building, fifth floor. I'll clear your visit. Ask for me."

"Jessup. Here to see Doctor Ayana." He offered his driver's license to the guard at the entrance to the Johnson Space Center.

The guard made a call, after which he lifted the gate and motioned Doctor Jessup into the space center property.

Doctor Jessup drove among modern buildings until he came to the tallest structure. While in the elevator to the fifth floor, his thoughts and emotions ran between fear for Bobby and anger at the man he had thought was his friend.

He exited and saw Doctor Ayana waiting in the hall. Doctor Jessup pointed a finger at the mathematician but caught himself before unleashing vitriol.

Doctor Ayana started the discussion. "Before we go in, I want you to know no one applied any pressure to Bobby. We gave him the tour, introduced him to some of our astronauts, and explained the situation." He placed a hand on Doctor Jessup's shoulder. "He wants to go. Really."

"Can I see him now?" Doctor Jessup's eye contact had become a glare.

Doctor Ayana led the way to a conference room where Bobby talked with two men wearing the blue uniforms of the astronaut corps.

"Doctor Jessup. I am so glad you are here." Bobby was all smiles as he sprang from his chair to give the man a bear hug.

"Bobby, I need to talk with you," Doctor Jessup said without introducing himself to the astronauts.

"And I want to talk with you. I'm so excited. The most wonderful thing happened. NASA wants to train me for an important space mission. I mean, really big stuff. Save the world kind of stuff. And me, over all the top people, even astronauts. Wow."

"I know, Bobby, but we need to discuss the mission. It is, to be honest with you, very dangerous. And I want to make sure you completely understand the risks and accept them freely."

"Doctor Jessup, they showed me the spaceship. So cool. Even let me sit in the pilot's seat. Has a super fast antigravity drive. And lasers that work. They can blast space rocks away. The controls are neat, too. No joystick. You control it with your thoughts, kind of like that calculus video game, but for real."

Bobby's eyes were bright, but his gaze averted to the window, as though his mind were somewhere else, probably considering the technology he had seen inside the pyramidal craft intended to carry him to the edge of the universe.

CHAPTER 14

"Your Honor." NASA's attorney, Angelo Martini, stopped his introduction to study a document for a moment. "We have provided a list of authorities in this brief to support our motion to abate the action before you on the basis that the plaintiff has no standing to bring such a case."

"I have read your brief, counsel," federal judge Oscar Horwitz said. "Response from the opposition?"

"Thank you, Your Honor." Attorney Alice Rendell peered over thin-frame glasses perched on the tip of her pointy nose. "I represent the Society for Disabled Citizens, a 501(c) nonprofit corporation that supports the rights of special-needs people."

"I am familiar with the organization's work, Miss Rendell. Its reputation is excellent," Judge Horwitz said with a nod of approbation.

"We have filed this case on an emergency basis to protect a young man with Down syndrome, Bobby Alderson, who has been conscripted by government agents representing NASA to fly a dangerous space mission for which he has no training or ability and from which he most likely cannot return. It is, in reality, a suicide mission. We seek an injunction from the court to stop this ill-conceived conscription and return Bobby to his school and the care facility where he belongs. NASA's attempt to abate our case by denying our legal right to bring such litigation on Bobby's behalf is without merit."

"Mr. Martini, she has a point. This court is inclined to protect the rights of special-needs citizens. Any rebuttal for NASA?" Judge Horwitz asked.

"Indeed, Your Honor. First, Bobby Alderson is not a special-needs person. He was genetically cured of his Down syndrome and now enjoys an IQ in the extraordinary range, perhaps even increasing. Second, he is an adult at eighteen years of age. Third, he was never conscripted but, rather, voluntarily went to NASA to consider this mission, for which he is uniquely qualified. Therefore, the movant has no legally justiciable interest in Bobby Alderson, who is not now disabled and, therefore, has no need for its well-intentioned but, in this case, misguided efforts to protect him."

"Miss Rendell, any response?" Judge Horwitz leaned across his desk and focused on her, obviously interested in the feisty attorney's retort to Martini's factual remarks.

"Your Honor, with all due respect to the good people of the National Aeronautics and Space Administration, what you just heard is misleading. Although Bobby is eighteen and has had genetic treatment to raise his IQ, he still has Down syndrome and lives in a special-needs facility with caregivers. The fact is that his emotional state and experience levels are not those of a normal person. He simply does not have the tools to make a life-and-death decision like this one. In fact, he says he loves everybody, even the kids who bullied him. Additionally, he is an orphan and needs someone to protect him, and that is our job, no matter what his chronological age might be. Special-needs classification is a lifelong condition."

"All right, I have heard enough. The court finds that the Society for Disabled Citizens has standing to bring this action. Therefore, NASA's motion to abate is denied. Miss Rendell, you may proceed on the merits of your case."

"Excuse me, Your Honor." A rugged-looking middle-aged man said before she could speak. He stood in the gallery and waited to be recognized by the court.

"Yes, and who are you, sir?" Judge Horwitz asked.

"Lynn Barbuda, assistant attorney general from Washington. I was waiting for the disposition of NASA's motion to abate. However, since it was denied and the case will proceed on the merits, I request permission to present my motion."

"That is highly irregular, counsel. Our rules require presentation of motions in writing prior to the hearing."

"I understand, Your Honor, and that is common practice in most courts. However, my motion is special because it concerns national security and falls under the Espionage Act as well as other federal laws. I could not reduce the motion to writing due to its sensitive content but must present it in person at this time."

"The Espionage Act, you say." Judge Horwitz rubbed his temple. "Now, that is heady stuff. You may proceed, counsel."

Barbuda approached the bench and said, "This case involves classified material from our scientific, space, and military programs. If made public, such material could aid our enemies and adversely impact the public. We, therefore, request that the case proceed under the rule, these proceedings be held in secret, the record be sealed, all participants be admonished under federal law they are to hold in strictest confidence everything they learn here, all nonparties be excluded, and all nonessential personnel be excused from the case." Attorney Barbuda's tone and expression reflected the seriousness of his comments and the authority of his office.

A young woman stood and addressed the court. "Your Honor. I am Delica Younts, attorney for the United News Organizations of America. We are here because of our members' First Amendment rights to gather and report news to the public. We believe this matter is of global importance and the government is using national security as a smokescreen to deprive the people of their right to know the truth about something that can profoundly affect them."

Judge Horwitz grasped his head between both hands. "Not another lawyer. For Pete's sake, what is this, Death by a Thousand Lawyers Day?" He snorted. "Mr. Barbuda, without disclosing secret details, why is this case a matter of national security?"

"Your Honor, I request a closed hearing in chambers with only the parties' attorneys, and, if I am correct, then you can take the steps we have requested. Otherwise, you can proceed normally with a public hearing."

"Very well. We will take a brief recess for a hearing in chambers. Only attorneys for NASA, the nonprofit, and Justice Department. No one else, including the court reporter and my clerk."

Delica Younts spoke sharply. "Excuse me, Your Honor, but we object on the basis of the First Amendment. Our constitution trumps all other law, even the Espionage Act. We should be allowed to attend the closed-door hearing to protect the rights of our organization as surrogate for the people."

The judge gestured with his hand as if to calm her. "Counsel, no jurist respects the constitution more than I do. However, if this truly is of national security significance, as the assistant attorney general alleges, then the press will just need to take a back seat. In the event this matter does not involve national security, then you will have full access to the proceedings and to the record for appellate purposes."

She sat wearing the most disagreeable expression.

The judge and invited attorneys retired to his chambers.

After about twenty minutes the attorneys and Judge Horwitz returned. He settled in his leather chair, his forehead wrinkled and face a bit ashen. For a moment, everyone who had been in the judge's chambers for the hearing seemed somewhat dazed: silent demeanor, pained expressions, and temporary indolence, until the judge collected himself and said, "All right. Mr. Barbuda's motion is granted. All counsel, parties, witnesses, and staff are hereby sworn to secrecy under the

Espionage Act and the National Secrets Act. All witnesses and party representatives are to leave the courtroom and wait in the hall until called and are hereby ordered not to discuss this case with anyone except me. The news organizations' motion for intervention is denied. This courtroom is to be cleared of all nonessential personnel, except for the parties' attorneys and the assistant attorney general, and the bailiff will maintain strict personnel control at the door. The record will be sealed. These proceedings are hereby ordered to be secret."

People exited the courtroom, including the scowling news organization lawyer, leaving only the NASA attorney, the attorney for the Society of Disabled Citizens, the assistant attorney general, and limited court staff.

"Excuse me, Your Honor. President Ballieu has requested that she be kept apprised of these proceedings since she is involved in the subject matter. May I disclose otherwise secret information to her?" Barbuda stood as he waited for a response.

"Very well, so ordered. You may keep her informed, but her only, not one of her aides or staff. Miss Rendell, please call your first witness," the judge said.

"Plaintiff calls Doctor Theodore Jessup," she announced.

The bailiff summoned Doctor Jessup from the hallway. He was sworn and seated.

"Doctor Jessup, do you know Bobby Alderson?" Rendell asked.

"Yes."

"What is your relationship with him?"

Doctor Jessup explained meeting Bobby as a subject for his genetic engineering work.

"Excuse me, sir, but was your project approved by the FDA? I don't remember reading anything about it," the judge said.

"Yes, it was, Your Honor. The project was not reported to the press for fear it might not work on humans and would then cause great disappointment among the families of afflicted persons."

"I see. Please continue."

Doctor Jessup discussed details of the project, his positive result with Bobby, the science behind the project, subsequent testing, and Bobby's enhanced IQ.

"Finally, Doctor Jessup, is Bobby normal in all respects, such as with respect to emotions and life skills?" Rendell asked.

"No. He lacks development in those areas."

"Can he live on his own, like you or I would?" she inquired.

"I don't think so."

"Why?"

"Well, he is so very trusting that everyone is good and life will turn out well. I am afraid some unscrupulous people might take advantage of him. He lacks real-life seasoning and experience to make the right decisions." Doctor Jessup glanced at the judge.

"Pass the witness," she said.

Martini then got his turn at cross examination and pounced like a cat on a mouse. "Isn't it true Bobby's IQ is increasing and recently tested at 196?"

"Yes."

"And that his mind is developing very rapidly, as though making up for lost time?"

"I suppose you could put it that way."

"And that his social skills are excellent in that he gets along with everyone?"

"As far as I know, he does."

"And that he is doing extremely well in high school socially and academically?"

"I haven't looked at his report card, but his teacher told me he makes all As."

"Objection, hearsay," Rendell said.

"I'll allow it since the information is from a trusted source. Proceed, Mr. Martini."

"Thank you, Your Honor. And isn't it a fact that Bobby has many friends and admirers among the other students?"

"Correct."

"And he is planning on going to college on scholarship by his own choosing?"

"That's right."

"And, that as far as you can tell, he volunteered for this mission and was not pressured?"

"Well now, I don't know that you could say he was not pressured," Doctor Jessup said.

"What pressure was applied?" Martini shot back.

"He was given a VIP tour of Johnson Space Center, showed the spaceship, allowed to sit in the pilot's seat. They even introduced him to some astronauts." Doctor Jessup stared hard at Martini.

"Then, you are saying that touring NASA, seeing space hardware, and meeting astronauts constitutes undue pressure, is that right?"

"It could be for an impressionable child, especially if the astronauts pressured him in some way, possibly only subtly; but that would still be undue influence."

"Bobby Alderson is not a child. He is an adult with superior intelligence, correct?"

"Yes, but . . ."

"Who has made his own decisions about going to college and majoring in mathematics and making the friends he chooses. Isn't that correct?"

"I suppose so."

Martini was on a roll. "And in fact you asked Bobby whether he wanted your genetic engineering treatment for his Down syndrome in the first place, and he gave you that permission, isn't that right?"

Doctor Jessup's head fell. "Yes," he said softly.

"And as far as influence goes, sir, you went to the Johnson Space Center uninvited and tried to influence him to not go on this mission, isn't that correct?"

"Yes, but it was for his own good."

"His own good. What about the good of the billions of innocent people on this earth who do not even know they will die in a matter of months if our country fails to stop this approaching cataclysm? What about them, sir? Aren't they worth our best effort?" Martini's litigation prowess was on full display.

"Objection," Rendell said. "There has been no foundation laid about the space phenomenon. The witness isn't qualified to speak on the subject."

Martini shot back, "Your Honor, we heard about the phase transition in your chambers. I am just trying to elicit proper testimony from this witness. Doctor Hassif Ayana, a scientist with NASA, is on the witness list. He can provide scientific details later."

"Overruled. I think we all understand what the earth is facing. I would like to hear this witness's response to the question. Please answer, sir."

Doctor Jessup did not say anything at first, after which he exclaimed, "All human life is precious."

"Exactly, sir, and we are talking about trying to save all of humanity on this planet. Don't you agree?"

"I do."

"Pass the witness," Martini said.

"Any redirect, Miss Rendell?" Judge Horwitz asked.

"No."

"Then call your next witness," the judge said. "Doctor Jessup, please remain in the courtroom. We may need clarification from you. However, you may not discuss this case with the other witnesses or anyone outside this courtroom."

"I understand, Your Honor."

"Doctor Hassif Ayana," Rendell said.

The witness walked from the hall and took his seat.

"What are your academic and professional credentials, Doctor?"

The mathematician gave a summary of his curriculum vitae.

"You are employed by NASA as a consultant?"

"I am."

"And wasn't it you who told the director of NASA about Bobby Alderson's special abilities?" she asked.

"I was the one."

"And you led federal agents to take Bobby from his school to the Johnson Space Center for a special briefing on this top-secret mission. Isn't that true?"

"Yes."

"Wouldn't you say that the briefing was intended to impress him about the importance of the mission and of his unique ability to fly it successfully?"

"I don't know about the briefing being intended to influence him. We only wanted to present him with the facts. Those include the calamity facing our universe, the spacecraft that will fly the mission to stop the danger, and Bobby's special talent to do the job. That's all. Nothing more." His tone was defensive.

"Doctor Ayana, could you please tell the court as concisely as possible the nature of the cosmic phenomenon threatening our universe and NASA's plan to reverse it?"

He explained the phase transition, its effect on the universe, the new heavy element, the first mission and its failure, and the need for a manned mission to maximize the chance of success. Whether it was the crushing substance of his explanation or the man's commanding presence, obvious intellect, or booming voice, the courtroom was gripped by his testimony.

"Why is Bobby Alderson uniquely qualified to fly this mission?" she asked.

"Because the genetic engineering that raised his IQ also seems to have sharpened all of his intellectual skills to an unprecedented level. He can do advanced math in his head, even spatial calculus. To my knowledge, no one else can do that. This skill is needed to navigate through space-time distortions and also to deliver the element to a precise target for reversal of the phenomenon. Our first mission, the unmanned one, failed because it did not hit the target. A computer alone probably is not responsive enough under the current chaotic conditions in deep space and may fail from intense radiation. Bobby, with his unusual mental skill, can probably do better."

"But, aren't there others who are intellectually qualified to fly the mission?" she asked.

"Yes, there are able astronauts, but none of them volunteered. At least, no able astronaut has given us unqualified agreement to go."

"Well, doesn't that tell you that they, as trained and experienced space travelers, see the impossibility of a mission like this?" Rendell said.

"I cannot say for sure why there were no unqualified volunteers. I didn't talk with them."

"But you can say with certainty that, after being informed of the details of this mission, there are no current astronaut or cosmonaut volunteers, isn't that correct?" She pounded the question home with strong emotion.

"Yes." He looked away.

Rendell sat. "Pass the witness, Your Honor."

Martini asked, "Doctor, there is a mathematical probability of this mission being successful, of saving our planet from destruction. Is that not correct?"

"There is."

"Pass the witness," he said.

Rendell shot up from her seat. "And, Doctor Ayana, please tell the court whether you have calculated the mathematical probability of the astronaut on this mission navigating the dangers of space to even reach this phase transition alive," she asked.

"I have."

"And what would that be, sir?"

"Well, there are several probabilities involved. The probability of the astronaut surviving until he reaches the phase transition region of space is 18.45 percent."

"And isn't it true the astronaut might die soon after arriving at the place where he will release the element, but before he can launch it, because of intense radiation in such an environment?" Her litigation skills were on fire as well.

"Yes. That is a possibility."

"And, if the astronaut becomes deathly sick from radiation soon after he arrives, then the mission might well fail because he may not be able to launch the element with the precision needed for success. In other words, in that likely case the mission will have been a waste, isn't that right?"

"You are correct, in that case."

"But, as a scientist, you know that radiation sickness is cumulative, meaning it gets worse over time, correct?"

"Yes." He sighed.

Judge Horwitz closed one eye to peer at the witness.

Rendell finished her questions.

"Any recross, Mr. Martini?" the judge asked in a raspy voice.

"Just a few. Doctor, what is the actual probability of this mission being a success, meaning that it stops the phase transition and saves our universe?"

"The mission's probability of stopping the phase transition is 9.06 percent. That is our current revised number based on new information," Doctor Ayana said.

Judge Horwitz leaned toward the witness. "Doctor, is there any chance that the astronaut can return safe to the earth from this mission?"

"Initially I thought not. However, recently our engineers discovered a method to enhance the plasma shield with the addition of a magnetic barrier to divert radiation, similar to the earth's magnetosphere. Interior radiation levels might be survivable. At least that is more possible now."

"Couldn't the pilot take something to ward off the effects of radiation, such as iodine?" the Judge Horwitz asked.

"We researched that possibility and concluded that all currently available radiation medicines will take too long to act and cannot protect against the extreme levels we expect near the transition boundary," the witness said.

"I see." The judge made notes.

Doctor Ayana paused and reflected, as though not finished.

"Is there something more that you would like to add?" the judge asked with obvious interest.

"Yes there is."

"Please enlighten us, sir."

"We had thought there would be no chance of the astronaut returning to earth. The enormous reaction of our element interacting with the phenomenon would be too great for craft survival. However, new calculations indicate there is some chance of a safe return from the concussion."

"How is that possible?" the judge inquired.

"If the element is delivered to the correct point, the resulting explosion might send our craft back across compressed space, akin to the recoil of a rifle. It will travel many times the speed of light. Assuming it can withstand the pressures and dangers involved, if the vehicle's orientation to the target is correct, it could be catapulted back across space on a course for a safe return to our solar system. From there, earth would be a hop, skip, and a jump for this craft."

"What is the probability that will occur?" The judge's elbows rested on the front of his desk.

"We calculate it to be 3.019 percent."

Judge Horwitz slumped in his chair. "Call your next witness."

"We rest," Rendell said.

"Will the defendant call any witnesses, Mr. Martini? I certainly can think of one critical witness." Judge Horwitz stared at NASA's attorney.

"I think we have the same person in mind, Your Honor. NASA calls Bobby Alderson."

Bobby bounced into the courtroom, all smiles. He saw Doctor Jessup and hugged him. "Hi, Dad."

Martini directed Bobby to the witness chair, and the clerk swore him in. The smile never left Bobby's face.

"Bobby, I am the attorney for NASA and I'd like to ask you a few questions. Is that all right?"

"You bet."

"Bobby, did you volunteer for this mission of your own free will? You do understand free will, don't you?"

"Oh, yes sir. Free will is like making your own decisions. Not being forced to do stuff you don't agree with. Saying what you really believe. Doing what you want to do, like being friends with someone who may not be cool."

Martini chuckled. "I think that about covers it. Better answer than I could give."

"Thanks," Bobby responded.

"So, Bobby, did you volunteer for this mission on your own, of your free will, rather than being made to go by some important adults?"

"Yes sir. I sure did."

"Was there anyone who forced you to volunteer or promised you something to do it?"

"Oh, no sir."

"Bobby, how old are you?"

"Eighteen, sir, last May."

"You were given a medicine by Doctor Jessup to correct your Down syndrome, isn't that right?"

"Yes. Six shots. One each week. It worked great. I'm real happy about it."

"Bobby, do you think that you are capable of making your own decisions now?"

"Yes. I am pretty smart, and I do good in high school. Better than most of the other smart kids, so far as I know."

"I pass the witness, Your Honor," Martini said.

"Miss Rendell?" Judge Horwitz asked.

She almost jumped from her chair. "Bobby, are you saying that you are completely grown up?"

"Oh no. I still have lots of growing up to do. Not physically, but in life."

"Don't you think that you need to get more experience before you can make serious decisions?"

"Depends. If you're talking about getting married, yes."

The judge laughed.

Bobby smiled in his direction and continued. "But if you're talking about stuff like what I want to do with my life, no. Lots of eighteen-year-old kids are like me. Some want to be doctors, others lawyers, still more want to be engineers or scientists. I want to be a physicist—theoretical physics, really. That's heavy on math. To study the secrets of the universe. How it formed. Dark Matter. What happens at the center of a black hole? Interesting stuff like that."

"I understand those decisions, Bobby, but I'm referring to life-and-death decisions. About things that are very important. Like a decision where you can't go back after you make it. What about them?"

"Well, aren't teenagers lifeguards? Some of them are on the beach with sharks and rip tides. They risk their lives to save other people. They're making life-and-death decisions, aren't they? And what about teenagers who volunteer for the army or navy?"

"I have no more questions, Your Honor," she said as Rendell settled in her chair.

The judge took control of questioning. "Bobby, do you understand this space mission has a significant chance that you will die?"

"Yes, sir. They told me about that."

"Then why did you volunteer for it, especially since your life as a normal person is just beginning?"

"Because it gives me the chance to save other people. What better job is there? I could become a doctor or a dentist maybe, and I would help people, but only some. This space mission is a chance to save the whole earth, all the people, and the animals too." He leaned toward the judge and whispered. "And, if there are intelligent aliens out there, it's a chance to save them also. Who could turn down a job like that?"

The judge blinked several times. "But, what if you die, Bobby, way out there in space all by yourself?"

"That's no big deal. I won't be alone. God will be there with me. And know what?"

"What?" the judge asked, seemingly captivated by Bobby's unbridled sincerity and powerful logic.

"He doesn't care that I'm a Downs kid. I'm His son, just the same as other people. Isn't that great?"

"Bobby, where did you learn about God?" the judge asked.

"From preacher Corbin at Bright Lighthouse. Real nice man." He stopped and made brief eye contact with the other people in the room, before he settled on the judge. "Told me that God loves me as much as everyone else and is with me always." Bobby's smile left him for a moment. "Some of the kids at school make fun of me for believing in God and say He doesn't exist. They care about celebrities and sports stars and movie heroes. Others believe like I do. But the kids who don't believe, they will come around some day when they learn what's really important to them." His smile returned. "God is real, and He has a place in Heaven for everybody. Me too, no matter what."

"And why do you think that? I mean, what gives you this strong belief that God is there for you? That He will protect you," the judge asked.

"Because people saw His miracles, like Jesus beating death or healing sick people, and they wrote about those things in the Bible a long time ago. That's not comic book stuff. It's true, same as history books. Tells about the first Christians who knew they would be put in jail and killed by the Romans. But that didn't stop them from believing. They went everywhere to give people some good news, lift up their spirits, tell everybody about good stuff that happened so they would feel better. It's kind of like what I will be doing out in space. Trying to save everybody and send the people back here on earth good news that they are going to live and that their kids can grow up. Doesn't that give you hope, sir?"

Bobby was smiling more widely than before, and the judge was smiling with him.

CHAPTER 15

"That's right, Bobby, think about the operation you want the ship to perform," chief design engineer Charles Sorenson said. "Try to exclude other thoughts, especially those based on emotions. Just think coolly and calmly about one thing at a time. The neuron potentiality pickup will transmit your brain activity to the computer, which will activate the correct control. This is much more responsive than manual control of a machine."

"Okay, Mr. Sorenson. I'll try again."

Bobby's expression changed from tense determination to dispassionate focus. The spacecraft lifted slowly inside the Johnson Space Center hangar and hung motionless.

"Great, Bobby. Now let's move forward just a few feet," Sorenson said.

Bobby thought; the craft moved forward and stopped.

"Fantastic. Now go backward a little."

Bobby concentrated; the craft reversed and stopped above its point of origin.

"Let's land under control, Bobby. Think you can do it?"

Bobby's expression remained blank but intent.

The craft settled gently on the floor.

"How was that?" Bobby was beaming.

"It was perfect. You're learning really fast. I should have seen that coming since you completed the simulator training so quickly. If you keep doing this well, soon we'll let you take her for a spin outside. Nothing too far. Maybe a series of places to test your navigational skills."

"That would be so cool. But what about space? When do I go there?"

"That's a couple weeks from now, when you have good command of the entire machine."

The following week an overcast night sky produced rain, as the weather service had predicted. It was a perfect stealth environment for the craft's third test flight, just in case amateur astronomers might have trained their telescopes on the heavens. Bobby was at the controls, mentored by Captain Julia Winslow, an experienced spacecraft pilot.

"We'll make this run with the Lominum crystals off. Their blue glow might cause all kinds of UFO panic. We've got to maintain secrecy," she said.

"Okay." He glanced at the Lominum crystal display. It showed the system to be off. "Great. I'm ready to go."

"Let's not get ahead of ourselves, Bobby. Remember to go through your protocol first to make sure everything is done properly for our flight."

"Oh, right. Guess I got a little excited." He went from left to right, top row first, checking every readout, followed by a review of the computer data on the ship's view screen.

"Now mentally acknowledge your review results to the computer for confirmation," she advised.

Bobby cerebrated, and the screen quickly showed a message in green letters: "Protocol review confirmed. All systems ready for liftoff."

"Now we can go," she said.

Bobby focused. The craft rose and moved silently through open hanger doors. It was dark against the night sky. In a microsecond the craft was gone, as though it never had existed.

Captain Winslow reiterated the operation of various pieces of equipment. She looked at the view screen. "Okay, we're over San Diego. Now slow the craft to five hundred miles an hour. Just think of that speed and the ship will respond immediately."

Bobby thought; the ship slowed.

"Let's navigate the mountain peaks. You can see them in red on the view screen. Use your mind to calculate elevations, vectors, and slopes with the data projected for each peak as shown on the screen. When you get the final answer, merely think 'transmit' and the pickup will relay that information to the control center."

The spacecraft pitched, yawed, and turned around peak after peak, rising and falling to follow the contours of the land.

It avoided outcrops, hills, and trees.

"That's terrific, Bobby. You've got it. Now turn southeast and hug the coast. Resume our original speed, and you'll see Guatemala City in a few minutes on the view screen. Then turn north to Houston."

Bobby concentrated and flew a perfect route. Within a short time the craft glided silently, steadily, precisely into the hanger at Johnson Space Center and came to rest on the floor.

Captain Winslow was smiling as Bobby opened the outer door by his thoughts.

"Are you proud of me?" he asked.

"Very. And I have a special surprise for you."

"What?" His eyes were wide with anticipation.

"Tomorrow night we lift off for the moon. If that goes well, next week it's the rings of Saturn." She patted his shoulder. "Excited?"

"You bet. That's so cool."

"Moon coming up, Bobby. We need to slow to orbit velocity. See it there on the readout?" Julia Winslow pointed to a series of numbers. "Use them to calculate orbit angle of attack, entry attitude, velocity, and altitude."

"Right."

The bright lunar landscape moved across the view screen. Oceanus Procellarum, Copernicus Crater, Mare Tranquillitatis, and Mare Fecunditatis were prominent. Twilight began to replace the intense illumination on the screen.

"Bobby, now you are going to see something incredible and unknown by the public. It's classified information disclosed to only a few people in the government."

The view screen went blank.

"We're going around the dark side. Activate the electron and infrared sensors. Max resolution," she said.

The screen showed a new picture, light green background with dark green outlines of craters, mountains, and maria.

"Increase magnification, Bobby. See the scale lines? They will give you a sense of the size of what you are about to see."

The view of natural features changed to distinct shapes of something far different. He gawked at soaring towers, some of which were cones and others rectangles; round structures each a half-mile wide; immense canals leading to pits; a low-rise square edifice with sides running for miles; wide roads; cranes jutting up from deep craters; massive excavators; hulking vehicles hundreds of yards long; elevated conveyor belts connected to buildings that produced heat signatures.

Captain Winslow pointed to one of the glowing buildings. "Nuclear material. Uranium 238 decaying. They used the heat to process minerals."

"They?" Bobby asked.

"Aliens. Built this place about ten thousand years ago. Then left. We don't know why. Abandoned the entire project. Equipment and all, except for the minerals they mined."

"Wow, aliens. Then they really do exist. Cool."

"Sure do, but our expedition wasn't able to determine where they came from. Not this solar system, that's for sure."

"Man, it would be so neat to meet them. Learn their technology. Make friends. I bet they could help us."

The scene changed to natural landmarks as the spacecraft emerged from the dark side of the moon.

"Okay, Bobby, let's head for earth now. Notice the return data on the computer screen."

"Piece of cake. I'll factor for orbit position and velocity, space drift from solar wind, planet rotation, and bingo, we're there in a flash." Bobby shot her a reassured expression.

A siren sounded, followed by a mechanical voice. "Danger, danger. Sensors detect foreign object. Position 102 by 678; speed 17,490 miles per hour; potential intersect in five minutes and thirty-three seconds; recommend avoidance measures."

Bobby changed the view screen to deep space mode and enhanced resolution.

Captain Winslow gripped the edge of the console. "Shit. Space junk. Several pieces traveling together. Bobby, we need to change course now."

He did not respond but exhibited the steely focus of a seasoned pilot many years older. His eyes became slits; his forehead wrinkled; the spacecraft vectored to starboard, rose three degrees, yawed on its side.

"Bobby, no wild gyrations. They could throw us off course, maybe into some greater danger, like burning up in the earth's atmosphere."

"I know, Captain Winslow." His expression never changed. "I got this."

The conglomeration of space junk grew larger in the view screen. There was no avoiding it. Their spacecraft was headed for a collision, until it scooted between pieces of entangled, jagged metal. The view screen immediately changed to rear imaging. The field of space junk was far behind and fading fast.

Captain Winslow's couldn't talk for lack of breath. She inhaled deeply and coughed before saying, "Bobby, that was fantastic. Looks like you need only one more trial run."

"Great. I'll bring her in to Johnson in exactly twenty-one minutes, Lominum crystals off. Don't want to cause a lot of false UFO sightings. Guess we can recharge gravitons in the hanger." He smiled at her. "But we know UFOs are real. Just our little secret, right?" He winked.

She winked back. "Ready for our next trip?"

"Where?" he asked.

"The rings and moons of Saturn. Two days from now. We'll navigate the outer ring material. It's mostly frozen water ice with rocks, pebbles, and dust. Then we'll do flybys of Saturn's moons. That should complete your training. If you can successfully navigate those gravitational forces and the ring material, you can do anything."

"All right, Bobby. Saturn in about six minutes. Now look at your readout data," Captain Winslow said.

Bobby glanced at a series of numbers on the view screen. "Okay. Gravity, solar wind drift, angle of attack, entry attitude, angular momentum."

"Good. The outer rings are coming fast. Compute your turn vectors and velocity to come in between the top two layers of material about one kilometer inside the edge. Remember to maintain orbital velocity."

Bobby concentrated on the view screen and became silent in thought, until he said, "Got it." His expression became blank as the craft slowed and turned toward Saturn's rings. In a few seconds it was flying in a void between ice fields stretching beyond the scope of his sensors. Icy boulders zoomed past, some about a meter in size while others seemed as large as a city bus. Toward Saturn the ring material became a white haze akin to a vast snow field.

Seven hundred kilometers ahead two massive boulders collided, sending shards of dirty ice into space.

"Bobby, now would be a good time to get some experience with the lasers," she said.

"Okay. What is their range?" he asked.

"Depends on the size of the incoming and its material. Look at that data on the screen." She pointed to several lines of numbers. "As you see, the computer is telling us this is ice with some silicates varying in size from sand grains to about one meter."

"When should I shoot?" he asked with eyes focused on the bright dots growing larger on the view screen.

"The sensors will give you a signal to activate lasers when the target comes within range for the lasers to be effective." She placed a hand on his shoulder. "Radar will lock on. You must think to energize the lasers."

The computer made a beeping sound.

"That's the signal to fire, Bobby."

Bobby focused, and the twin lasers shot powerful beams of photons into the closing shards, vaporizing many of them. Their ship penetrated the remaining debris field undamaged.

"Way to go, Bobby. Remember that you can divert power temporarily from the engines to the lasers for more destructive energy, if necessary. You must concentrate on that feature when you need it."

"I'll keep that in mind. I guess we could have also increased our plasma shield to get through," he said.

"Maybe, but I would not rely on plasma as a weapon to save the ship. That's only for radiation and pebbles. Better to use the laser to destroy something that's about to collide with you."

"Okay. Great advice. Glad you're my teacher."

She patted him on the back. "Glad you're such a good student."

Bobby climbed out of the rings and completed one orbit around the gas giant before heading toward Saturn's largest moon, Titan. The yellow atmosphere and stable bodies of surface water made Titan unique among rocky moons. They made a close pass by Dione, its soaring ice cliffs apparent on the view screen. Frozen water erupted from volcanoes on Enceladus.

Bobby noticed sunlight-illuminated ice particles from an Enceladus volcano rising high into space to form a crystal river that ended in one of Saturn's rings. "Wow, look at that."

Captain Winslow pointed to the river and said, "Enceladus feeds that ice field. That's one way it formed."

The spaceship sped past irregularly shaped Hyperion, continued around the dramatic colors of Lapetus, dipped toward the massive impact crater on Mimas, and soon left the remaining moons—Rhea, Tethys, and Phoebe—far behind as it streaked to earth. A bright dot ahead grew into the blue planet.

Bobby considered his home with tenderness. "Gosh, it's so beautiful. I'll be glad to get back and feel the sun on my face."

"Bobby, are you having second thoughts about this mission? Do you now want to stay with your friends on earth rather than go into space?" She waited for his response, possibly believing the young man was homesick, perhaps to the extent of scrubbing the mission.

"Oh no, Captain Winslow. It's nothing like that. I was just thinking how happy I am back home. How beautiful it is. Lots of other people must feel that way, too. I never want the earth to go away."

The mood at Johnson Space Center was festive. General Jackson chatted with Bobby. Doctor Ayana laughed with several astronauts. The navy band played jaunty music.

A voice came over the public address system: "Ladies and gentlemen, the president of the United States."

A large monitor showed President Ballieu seated on a sofa in the Oval Office. She had chosen a very patriotic red, white, and blue dress. Her bright eyes and broad smile were reminiscent of a proud grandparent. She leaned toward the camera and said, "Bobby, I want to express the gratitude of our entire nation to you and to the team members who prepared for this critical mission. When it is successfully completed, I will announce to the world the incredible feat you will have achieved, nothing less than the survival of our species. Bobby, we love and respect you. I pray that God will be with you throughout your journey and keep you strong."

The crowd clapped, whistled, and cheered. General Jackson shook Bobby's hand. Others patted him on the back. Doctor Ayana stood taller than usual.

Doctor Jessup frowned, shook his head, and mumbled. "Taking advantage of an unsophisticated kid for a suicidal feel-good mission that can't succeed. Horrible. Where is our soul?"

The guests mingled, talked, and ate catered barbeque. The band changed to easy-listening music.

General Jackson greeted a newly arrived guest. "Senator, welcome. Good to see you made it."

"Happy to be here. Just finished with the Russian delegation. I think the secretary and I have them calm, at least for now. They're so paranoid about this mission turning into a military thing against them. Success will fix a lot of problems, though." Senator Millstone scanned the room. "I sure want to meet the star of the show. Where is he?"

"Yes, indeed," the general said. "That is Bobby Alderson. Let me get him." General Jackson glanced around the room. "Where could he be?" He turned to an aide. "Have you seen Bobby?"

"He left with someone. Doctor Jessup, I believe."

General Jackson's forehead wrinkled. "He can't leave the center. Our mission lifts off in two days. He's supposed to go into quarantine tonight. Find him right now."

General Jackson sat glumly at the conference table across from FBI special agent Margo Withers. He cursed. "I don't understand it. How could he just take off like that? Bobby seemed so eager to go on the mission. He understands its importance and how critical he is to our success."

"It wasn't Bobby, General. Most likely Jessup is trying to persuade him to abandon the mission. Some people say Jessup was opposed to Bobby going, that he thought the government was taking advantage of an emotionally unprepared young man." She looked hard at him. "Truth is, General, Bobby was kidnapped."

"I should have prevented this and secured Bobby. Kept Jessup away. Of course I knew he wasn't happy with us, but I didn't think he would actually do anything, only that Jessup was a complainer. Can you find Bobby?"

She grinned. "We can. The question is whether he has been compromised for this mission."

"Compromised?"

"Bobby's emotional state. Will he still be as willing as before? Jessup may be able to change his mind. After all, Bobby thinks of the man as a father figure. An unwilling astronaut is of no real use to anyone. Don't you agree, General?"

He looked at the floor for several seconds, then directly into her eyes. "There is no one else. It's Bobby Alderson or we turn out the lights. He must go, and we've got to hope Jessup hasn't messed with his mind." He snorted. "Look, I know Jessup isn't a bad guy, but he's probably not thinking clearly. I was warned by Ayana that Jessup is emotionally involved with Bobby. Sees him almost as a son. Ayana also said Jessup might believe the transition is mainly theoretical and that Bobby's life is being wasted for nothing. That Jessup's work is also being wasted." Another thought quickly occurred to the general. "All that aside, we've got to move fast. How can you locate him quickly? Our launch window is narrow. This phenomenon is disrupting the universe more each day. The scientists say we launch within two days or forget it. Our spacecraft won't be able to survive the journey after that."

"DNA sniffer dog drones," she said.

"Never heard of them."

"Top secret technology. We unleash, no pun intended, a swarm of micro drones. They are called dogs because the drones look like terriers. Very realistic so they don't raise suspicion. We program the missing person's DNA into their nose computers. They're very good at sniffing out someone's location. Better than a bloodhound. Usually goes pretty fast, no more than one day. A person leaves a DNA scent trail and the dogs find it real quick. Made the criminals go nuts. Crime statistics have plunged." She laughed. "They had to get jobs."

Doctor Jessup closed the hurricane shutters, somewhat muffling the sound of waves on Galveston Island's west beach, but not for storm protection. Rather, he wanted to shield the interior from prying eyes. Doctor Jessup turned on the television and selected a local news channel. After a moment, he whispered to himself. "Nothing about Bobby. That's not surprising. Everything is hush hush. Good for us."

Bobby came in from the deck facing the Gulf. "Doctor Jessup, I'm glad to be here. Neat place. Those lights way out on the water must be ships."

"Oil rigs and work vessels. Some are shrimp boats," he said.

"Cool. Never seen a house like this before. Thanks, and I liked the burger and fries a lot." He looked at the front door. "I really should get back. They'll be looking for me. You know, the mission and all."

"Bobby, that's just it. I wanted to talk with you without the others."

"Why?" Bobby asked. "Is there some problem with them? They're not spies are they?"

"No, nothing like that. I just want to make sure you understand the risks involved with this mission."

"Oh, I understand."

"Do you, Bobby, really?"

Bobby cocked his head.

Doctor Jessup's tone became soft and compassionate. "I'm not with NASA, which means I care about you rather than some government program. Doctor Ayana is a good man, but he's also a NASA scientist, and he told me about this mission. It's what they call a suicide mission,

Bobby. Do you understand how serious that is, now that you're away from all the NASA hype?"

"That most likely I will die."

"Correct. But, for what? Ayana said the chance of success is very small. You will travel much farther than any manned mission has ever gone. Things are really dangerous in deep space, and we have no experience there."

Bobby looked up at him. "I love you, Doctor Jessup. And I trust you. Like when you gave me those shots. I guess I'm a little confused right now."

He held Bobby close for a tender moment before grasping the young man's shoulders at arm's length and making eye contact. "Bobby, do you know how we got funding for our work to correct your genetic defect? That research cost over a hundred million dollars. We couldn't get much government money. Some of the congressmen and their advisors said our research was a waste and that we should focus on more worthwhile projects. That really upset me because I knew genetic engineering has such great potential, not just for people with Downs but for millions of people with all kinds of genetic defects." His breathed deeply to prepare himself for painful emotions. "I thought our team would never be able to do the project. It was really depressing."

Bobby patted his arm. "You must have been upset. I'm sorry for that."

"I was, but then I approached Mr. Edmond Green. Have you heard of him?"

"Yeah, he's the man developing the flying car. Runs on free static electricity in the air. No charging necessary. Right?"

"That's correct. He wrote a book about his brother and their relationship as children. His little brother had Downs, like you were born with. Mr. Green wrote that some of the other kids picked on his brother because he was different. He even told about one time when his brother ran home terrified and shaking with a bloody nose. He felt so sorry for his brother that Mr. Green decided then and there to defend him wherever he went. Like a sort of guardian angel. And he did that until his brother's death from natural causes." Doctor Jessup paused and cleared his throat. "Mr. Green cares about people in need. He agreed to meet me and discuss our research. He became interested. Asked a lot of questions and visited our lab. After that, Mr. Green told me he wanted to fund our work to help other people afflicted with Down syndrome so that they would not have to endure what his brother went through."

"Sounds like he's really a terrific guy, like you, Doctor Jessup. He wants to help people by spending his own money. And you used it to fix me. Thanks." Bobby smiled as innocently as a child looking up at a familiar face.

Doctor Jessup returned the smile. "That's why I want you to live happily here on earth for as long as possible. Enjoy life during that time. Be a normal person and give others hope by showing them we can overcome genetic defects. That would honor Mr. Green's kindness. Besides, I don't really believe all of that phase transition nonsense anyway."

"Really? Why not?" Bobby asked.

"Because it seems theoretical, like dark matter and the end of the universe. Yeah, some scientists think those things are real, but there is no proof. It's all conjecture, guesswork. Many times, Bobby, scientists think up things so they can get their names out there and become famous. Some of them have even been known to fake scientific papers."

"But, Doctor, what about the astronomers? They have seen it."

"What are you talking about?"

"The destruction of planets and galaxies from a huge fire coming this way. There is something out there all right, and it's bad. Somebody's got to do something."

"Who told you about that?"

"The people at NASA. Even showed me pictures of a small galaxy. Here one minute as the fire approached; gone the next when the fire passed it by. I don't believe they faked those pictures." Bobby seemed to lose his boyish demeanor for a moment.

Doctor Jessup shook his jowls in frustration. "Even if the transition is true, maybe it won't get here for many years, like when our sun dies billions of years from now. You might be able to live a normal life before anything bad happens, and I can correct other Downs people so they can also be happy for years to come."

"Really? But how do we know that? And, shouldn't we plan for the worst, just in case the scientists are right? If they are, we can give it our best shot to save everyone on earth."

Doctor Jessup shook his jowls again. "Okay, suppose the scientists are correct. This phase transition might be God's way of erasing a troubled world to start over fresh, of getting rid of all the evil things here because we can't do it." He studied Bobby's face for a moment and said, "If we are all destined to die, at least you should have the opportunity to live as fully and happily as possible to the end, to enjoy life here with the people you love. Besides, who can go against God, anyway? You wouldn't try that, would you?"

"No, but . . ." Bobby swallowed nervous saliva away, as though not wanting to challenge his dear friend. "Do you believe that kind of stuff?"

"What stuff? I don't understand your question, Bobby."

"About God. That He wants to kill everyone. There are good people like Mr. Green and Miss Saunders and you. Wouldn't God be happy with people like that and want to save them to help lots more than just me? Because good people just do good stuff. They give money and work hard and stand up against bullies and go into dangerous places to help people stop suffering. Why would God hurt them?"

"Maybe He wouldn't want to harm good-hearted people. But so many terrible things have happened and are still occurring, causing people to suffer a great deal. Wars, dictators, slavery, concentration camps, mass killings, drug lords, organized crime, government corruption. And now, weapons that can make humans go extinct. Could be He's just fed up and lost patience with us all."

"I don't see how that could be true, Doctor Jessup. If God wanted to wipe out everyone, He'd just do it, zap. Why would He give us a chance to save the world? Doesn't that seem like He wants us to try? Maybe we can. Don't you think?"

"I, I suppose that could be." He ran a thumbnail across his jaw in reflection.

Doctor Jessup's thought process was interrupted by a commotion at the front door. He peered through the peephole but saw no one standing there. He cracked the door and gulped.

"Woof!" A vaguely metallic-sounding bark froze the man.

CHAPTER **16**

Phase Craft Two rested on a concrete pad at Ellington Field under the cover of a moonless night. General Jackson, Doctor Ayana, and other officials and scientists watched from Mission Control at the Johnson Space Center.

"Bobby, we are in final countdown. All systems are a go here," said the mission director, Sam Collins. "Please verify craft analog."

"Yes sir. Computers check one hundred by one hundred; plasma shield is one hundred by one hundred; magnetic barrier one hundred by one hundred; anti-graviton engine shows one hundred by one hundred function; thrusters one hundred by one hundred; life support is also one hundred by one hundred. All systems okay."

"Copy. Remember to disengage the Lominum crystals until you reach space. Then you can engage the system and continue charging gravitons. Also, boosted electromagnetic transmissions will be intermittent depending on space-time warping. Right now, we are receiving photons from the transition boundary almost in real time, but that has been known to change from time to time. If we don't respond to your radio communications, keep trying. Space-time will fluctuate and the signals may or may not get through," Collins said.

"I will do that, sir."

"Bobby, there is someone here who wants to speak to you. She just arrived."

"This is President Ballieu, Bobby. I wanted to be at Johnson for your launch. You are a hero, Bobby, as important to our nation as any hero who ever lived. Please remember that. And also we will be praying for your success and safe return. God speed, dear friend."

"Thank you. I'll try hard. May I ask you something?"

She quickly responded. "What is it?"

"Will you still think I'm a hero if I fail?"

"Bobby, you are already a hero, the bravest one I have ever known."

The countdown blared from a loudspeaker in Mission Control and on the spacecraft: "Ten, nine, eight, seven, six, five, four, three, two, one, liftoff."

The anti-graviton engines produced a bright flash, and the craft was gone, not even a light in the sky.

"Bobby, do you copy?" Sam Collins said as he watched the spaceship's ascent on radar.

Static cleared. "Yes sir. Copy. In orbit now. Preparing for slingshot to Mars." Bobby's voice was cheerful, as usual.

"Very good, Bobby. Our people there are expecting you. Land as directed and then report to Colonel Offington. His technicians will go over the ship for your jump to interstellar space. Should take about one day. Two tops."

Red hues of Mars dominated the view screen of Phase Craft Two. Bobby studied images of Olympus Mons as it grew incredibly massive with the spaceship's approach.

"Mars Base Alpha calling. This is Colonel Offington, base commander. We have you on radar, Phase Craft Two. Come in at coordinates 18.65 degrees north and 226.2 degrees east. You will see the landing lights at that point. Proceed through the entrance of the lava tube all the way to its end. We will secure the air lock once you set down at the landing pad. It's well marked and lighted. I will meet you there."

Phase Craft Two descended toward paired light strips leading to a gaping wound in the side of the ancient volcano. When he was a few meters from the surface, Bobby glided the spaceship into the mountain of dried lava. Bright arrows directed his progress through a warren of natural tunnels to a landing pad twenty-four kilometers within the interior. The spaceship settled on a concrete pad.

The ship's interior speaker came to life again. "Please wait until the airlock door is closed and normal atmosphere is established. Our personnel will then walk onto the reception dock and you may exit." The voice was not that of Colonel Offington, but sounded very official, nonetheless. Bobby obediently saluted and waited for people to appear in the view screen.

He smiled. "Bingo. Time to see some cool stuff and have lunch. Hope it's good. Maybe a cheeseburger."

He opened the spaceship's outer door and bounced up stairs, a smile on his face, to shake hands with two men. "Bobby Alderson. Sure glad to be here."

"I'm Colonel Offington. Happy to receive you, Bobby. We've been expecting your arrival. You'll be with us overnight while we check the ship. General Jackson asked that we make you comfortable. Are you hungry?"

"You bet." Bobby clapped with anticipation.

"We have a really good cafeteria here. Everyone seems to like it. They also make pizzas and burgers if you prefer them."

"I was hopin' you would say that. Burgers are great."

They entered a maglev vehicle and zoomed silently farther into the interior of the largest volcano in the solar system.

Colonel Offington seemed an enthusiastic tour guide. "These lava tubes are an excellent natural habitat for our personnel. The rock shields us from meteorites and radiation. Martian weather as well. Massive dust storms mostly. All we had to do was secure the interior for pressurization of an atmosphere we created with oxygen and nitrogen generators. After that, we assembled prefab structures for living quarters, medical clinic, research labs, hydroponics, a machine shop, and storage. It all went pretty fast. Took a little more than a year."

"You have a whole city here. How do you grow stuff without sunlight?"

"Farm lights. They produce the same wavelength as natural sunlight. We harvest varieties of fruits and vegetables. We even have a grass field for outdoor activities like soccer. I'll show you that later," Colonel Offington said proudly.

"You mean real grass? Thick and green like on a football field?"

Colonel Offington chuckled. "You can roll on it the same as on earth." He winked. "And not get any chinch bugs. We left them all back home."

Bobby laughed.

The colonel's smile faded as his eyes focused keenly on something ahead. The vehicle took a left turn down another lava tube. "Bobby, before we go to the compound, I want to show you something very interesting. We discovered it shortly after we started exploring these lava tubes. It took us about a year to build an elevator to the bottom. That's where the investigation is ongoing. It's puzzling."

After several minutes of travel, the vehicle came to a gentle halt. Colonel Offington led the way and waited for Bobby on a platform overlooking a wide chasm. Bobby peered across the void but could not see the other side. He leaned over a metal railing and followed lights running downward to a confusing mixture of light and shadows. No bottom was apparent. Bobby kneeled and ran his hand over the surface of the chasm wall. He did it again and scratched his head.

Bobby watched a football-shaped elevator car rise to the platform. A door slid open. Two men and two women clothed in white one-piece garments exited. One of the men approached Colonel Offington and extended a gloved hand holding a black rock. "It's 89 percent iron; 7 percent nickel; 4 percent trace metals, lead mostly," the man said as he looked at the rock.

"Bobby, this is Doctor Juan Garcia, from the University of Mexico City. He is a leading geologist and one of the planetary scientists working on the project."

"Glad to meet you, sir." Bobby peered over the railing again. "How far is it to the bottom?"

"About fifteen hundred miles. Takes us three hours. The elevator travels five hundred miles an hour using high output electrical motors," Doctor Garcia said.

"Whoa. Now there's an elevator that can haul."

"We're seated and buckled." The doctor glanced at the rock and said to Colonel Offington, "Still no uranium. Can't find a trace, not one becquerel." His face became contorted in a way that says, "I can't figure this out and it's killing my soul."

"Bobby, have you read much about Mars?" the colonel asked.

"Yes. I love reading science books. Mars is as old as the earth, but lost its atmosphere millions of years ago, probably because the iron core cooled and stopped turning. That caused the magnetic field to stop, which let radiation from the sun reach the planet and destroy most of its atmosphere. Surface water evaporated and life died, if there was life here. Mars became a cold desert. Is that correct, Colonel?"

"Indeed, you have the basic facts down well. But do you know why the iron core cooled, Bobby?"

"No sir. Don't remember reading anything about that."

Colonel Offington took the rock and rubbed it with his index finger. "Normally, a planet's iron core remains molten for billions of years because of the uranium, which is the heaviest natural element known. Heavy elements like uranium and iron sink to the center of the planet when it's forming. Uranium decays there and creates enormous heat, enough to melt the iron, which rotates as a liquid and creates a protective magnetic field around the planet. That's the way our earth is today." The colonel interrupted his explanation as he returned the rock to Doctor Garcia. "Somehow, all the uranium is gone on Mars. Core heating then stopped and the iron solidified. The core came to rest. As you said, that's when the magnetic field disappeared. What we can't figure out is what happened to the uranium. There is no way it became inert. Uranium 238 has a half-life of about 4,500,000,000 years, the same as on earth. So why is it still producing heat on our planet but not on Mars? That's the big question."

Doctor Garcia added, "Some of our scientists think Mars had a different isotope of uranium that reached half-life long ago and became inert shortly afterward. Something we have not encountered on earth." He rubbed his forehead. "But that seems unlikely. Uranium would still leave some radioactive trace, a nuclear fingerprint. We can't detect any atomic remnant. The uranium seems gone. Every trace of it."

Bobby stepped to the railing, gazed down the volcanic shaft once more, and craned his neck to peer into its upper darkness. "Aliens could have done it."

"Aliens?" Doctor Garcia's face became contorted again.

"Sure. They could have bored a hole through the rock crust to allow lava to flow to the surface, probably where Olympus Mons sits. Maybe the crust is thinner here."

"How would they do that, Bobby?" Colonel Offington asked.

"With a solar beam from a huge mirror in orbit around Mars. Of course the mirror would need to stay over one place. I think they call that a geosynchronous orbit. The mirror would focus light on one point and melt the rock. Keep the beam focused long enough on that spot and you could drill to the center of Mars."

"What makes you think aliens used a beam of light, Bobby?" Doctor Garcia seemed skeptical.

"This big hole." Bobby pointed to the chasm. "The side is smooth as glass and too straight to be natural. Volcanoes shoot lava to the surface through uneven chimneys and tunnels, because lava hardens into jagged rock. This hole is way different than that. This is like a missile silo I read about.

"Something like a beam of energy must have been used as a drill. Probably focused sunlight because it's free energy for the aliens. Heck, we use sunlight back on earth. Why not aliens on Mars?"

"And the uranium, what happened to that? Did the beam of sunlight destroy it?" the colonel asked, now seeming to be interested in his visitor's explanation.

"They mined the uranium from the fluid metal and rock that came up from inside Mars." He looked at them for some reaction but saw only wide eyes. "Since heat creates outward pressure, the fluids could rise in the tunnel so long as the aliens kept the hole open and shut off other ways out. Over time, the uranium was gone from them mining it on the surface. That's probably the reason Olympus Mons is so big. The lava just kept coming for thousands of years, running down the volcano and spreading out, like in Hawaii, only a lot bigger. The aliens took all the uranium from the lava but left everything else."

Colonel Offington glanced at Doctor Garcia and said, "Do you read a lot of science fiction, Bobby?"

"No, I've heard about it, but I never read a science fiction book or anything. I like science and math the most. Physics, calculus, hydrodynamics, string theory, and, of course, the Bible. Lots of good stuff in it. You just gotta open your mind, but it's there."

Doctor Garcia walked to the railing and peered down the shaft for several seconds. He retrieved his Geiger counter and ran it around the edge of the chasm. "Nothing, not even background. *Solo Dios sabe,*" he uttered. Doctor Garcia turned to study Bobby.

Colonel Offington placed a hand on his visitor's shoulder. "Right, well how about that lunch?"

CHAPTER 17

Bobby awakened to the sound of a voice coming from the spaceship's console speaker: "Warning. Gamma ray burst detected from NGC 4487. North Pole beam projected to intersect current course in fifty-nine minutes and thirty-six seconds. Alternative course recommended."

He switched on the view screen. A bright light dominated the upper right corner. NGC 4487 had gone supernova and was generating deadly gamma rays and X-rays from its poles as well as visible light.

"Deep space views north and south of NGC 4487."

The computer produced successive scenes: rocky planets orbiting a massive blue star; a red giant turning the surface of a tightly bound planet to molten rock; a white dwarf sucking mass and energy from a binary relative to live again; a yellow main sequence star, much like the sun, radiating energy to its captive planets and moons; a rapidly spinning pulsar casting an intense electromagnetic beam into the universe; a small group of red dwarfs burning dimly; and a black hole consuming nebula gas and dust to shine as a quasar from intense friction-generated heat.

"Man, some of those planets are probably in danger." Bobby hoped the beam would lose destructive power before it sterilized inhabited worlds. "Close-up view of solar system with planets in danger from NGC 4487's gamma ray burst."

The intense bright point had grown dark, allowing Bobby to see more clearly that group of planets illuminated by the yellow main sequence star previously viewed. Suddenly, the star's plasma atmosphere elongated laterally from the gamma ray burst. The star's superheated plasma consumed nearby planets. A more distant blue planet turned gray as the gamma ray burst blew its oxygen atmosphere into space.

Bobby's chest heaved. "Oh man. I hope if anyone lived there, they got away in time."

A gas giant akin to Jupiter roiled for a moment before its colorful gas shroud disappeared from the destructive energy beam.

Beyond the solar system other worlds lay in the path of the deadly column, waiting to be destroyed.

"Warning. Intersection with gamma ray burst in forty-nine minutes and six seconds. Immediate course change recommended."

"What is the diameter of the burst at the point of intersection?" Bobby asked.

The computer quickly responded. "Six hundred twenty thousand nine hundred miles."

Bobby sat in the pilot's seat and concentrated on the view screen. Phase Craft Two changed course several degrees.

The speaker came to life again. "Warning. New course will result in close encounter with magnetar."

"How close?"

"One million one thousand seventy-eight miles."

"Strength of magnetic field?" Bobby asked.

"Ten to the twelfth power tesla." After a moment of pause, the computer said, almost as an afterthought, "Sufficient to remove all information from my memory and destroy electronic components."

"Thanks. That's what I really needed to know."

"I realized that," the computer said.

Bobby whispered to himself. "Got to avoid that magnetar but stay on course." His voice rose. "Minimum safe distance from magnetar?"

The computer responded. "Two million ninety-nine thousand eight hundred miles."

Bobby's gaze grew intense, jaw muscles bulged, nostrils flared, before he remembered to remove emotion from his cerebrations. He calmly calculated a new trajectory to miss the gamma ray burst, avoid the magnetar, and return to original course. Bobby was at one with the machine, sending the spaceship on a new path that changed several times as Bobby's mental energy was converted into electronic commands the computer transmitted to the ship's engines.

Phase Craft Two glided through the cosmos free of the gamma ray burst and the magnetar's influence. Its flight was, at last, peaceful. Distant stars shone brightly. The transfixing scene lulled Bobby into slumber.

A concussive jolt yanked Bobby from sleep. "What's happening? Did we hit something?"

"It appears we are under attack from an alien spacecraft," the computer said.

"Attack? Why would aliens want to hurt us? We're not bothering anybody. This isn't an invasion. I hope they're smart enough to know that."

Another concussion shook Phase Craft Two and threw Bobby from his seat to the floor.

"Maybe not. Computer, put the alien ship on the view screen," Bobby said.

The screen changed pictures from deep space to an approaching spacecraft. Perimeter lights shone brightly on a diamond-shaped craft. The view screen scale measured it to be three hundred feet long. Its leading point shone red. The point brightened before emitting a blast of red energy. Phase Craft Two shuddered again.

"We probably entered some region of space where the aliens live. They do not recognize us and assume we are hostile, possibly because they are warlike beings," the computer explained.

"Show close-up of alien spacecraft," Bobby said as another concussion shook Phase Craft Two. He leaned closer to the screen.

"Look out," Bobby said as the point brightened. "They're gonna' shoot again." Bobby concentrated, quickly maneuvering Phase Craft Two to avoid another intense red beam.

"Will they destroy the ship?" Bobby asked the computer.

"For now, our plasma shield and magnetic barrier are holding. However, there is no assurance they can remain resistive for an extended period. The alien beam seems to be a charged particle weapon, electrons most likely. Our plasma shield degrades slightly with each attack and requires time to recharge fully."

"Man, this is a super crunch. Aliens for real, with ray guns to take us out. Computer, any suggestions to save the ship?"

"Yes, you could use our craft's pulse lasers. They may have sufficient power to breach the alien hull."

"Oh, I couldn't do that," Bobby answered quickly.

"Why not?"

"Because, there are living beings on that spacecraft and they probably have family back home. People who love them. Besides, I'm saving the universe for everyone, even the aliens. Computer, there's got to be another way," Bobby said as a concussion raised Phase Craft Two's internal temperature to an uncomfortable level.

"Bobby, we cannot withstand many more attacks. Our equipment will overheat and fail within a short time. We must act now. Attack or evade? The command is yours as captain of this vessel."

"Evade, you say. How?"

"I will put data on the view screen, Bobby. There is an especially strong gravitational wave coming this way. Our engines plus the force of that wave should catapult us light years away from here. Two point seven four light years to be precise. You will need to plot engine start time and course," the computer advised.

"Okay, let's get to it," Bobby said as a concussion turned the temperature readout to red. "Stop it, dude. Geeze, we got to get out of here pronto."

"I completely agree," the computer responded. "My circuits are overheating and will fail with one more strike from their weapon."

Bobby concentrated, and the gravitational wave reached Phase Craft Two. Its antigravity engines ignited, Phase Craft Two flashed forward beyond the speed of an approaching red blast that faded far behind the hurtling craft.

"I think we did it, computer. I don't see the aliens on the screen. Do you detect their ship?"

"No, Bobby. It is in another part of the universe. But, Bobby, there is something else."

"I hope it's not a second alien spaceship about to attack us or a gamma ray burst."

"No," the computer said.

"Then what?"

"I would like to say this in a way so as not to alarm you, Bobby, since you just experienced a trying emotional event. But . . . warning, warning. Hyper-nova ahead. S50014+379. Mass approximately forty million solar masses. We are being pulled in that direction by the star's gravity. Convulsive phases are occurring at this time. Catharsis of energy and matter will start shortly when the star explodes again."

Bobby jumped to his feet and studied the view screen. "Our sensors don't show anything bad coming toward us."

"The star's gravity has taken over for the moment, sucking energy and mass back into the core. However, intense heat from the star's collapse will send destructive electromagnetic energy and heavy elements into space. I calculate the star could explode at any time. In that event, gamma rays and X-rays can reach us in six minutes and thirteen seconds if we continue to approach the star, at which time we will be destroyed before our remnant atoms are drawn in."

After a moment the computer said, "Sensors just detected another explosion. Destructive energy on the way."

"Computer, can we use antigravity drive to repel from the star's gravitational pull?"

"Affirmative. However not fast enough to escape intense X-rays and gamma rays coming toward the ship. Craft destruction likely at five minutes forty seconds from now. We will need to use another gravity wave to achieve boosted escape velocity." A timer appeared on the view screen.

"Is there another one in our vicinity?" Bobby asked.

"There is. They are coming with some regularity. The next one is more powerful than the last; sufficient energy to send us beyond escape velocity and allow us to avoid the approaching radiation."

"When will the gravitational wave arrive?"

"Six point eight seconds before the radiation," the computer answered.

"Man, I got to be on my game for this one. Only about six seconds to spare." Bobby glanced at the timer.

"On my game?" the computer asked.

Bobby did not look up from the data displayed on the view screen but managed to say, "Yeah. Means do real good. No mistakes."

"I completely agree."

Bobby studied his star charts, mumbled a series of numbers, stared at the view screen data, and looked at the timer once again. His mind set a new course.

"Bobby, we had better go now. There are only 20 seconds left before craft destruction from radiation. Hopefully, the gravitational wave will catch us and thrust us forward."

"I know, computer. Hold on."

Seconds ticked away: nine, eight, seven. Suddenly, Phase Craft Two jolted from its position. Bobby was thrust into his seat and he said, "We're surfin' the wave."

"Surfin'?" the computer responded.

"You bet. Yeeha. Feel the power, computer?"

"As you say, yeeha."

The starscape changed on the view screen. Bright points blurred while others disappeared as gravitational lensing distorted cosmic optics. Phase Craft Two began to vibrate. Its antigravity engines hurtled the spaceship along a tangent Bobby had calculated to escape the star's deadly radiation and avoid empyrean bodies within three light years.

The view screen showed static before going dark. Onboard, time slowed. Bobby watched seconds come to a stop. Phase Craft Two's automatic pilot maintained course.

"We must be traveling real fast, faster than even before, many times the speed of light. Computer, how long before we reach a safe distance from the hyper-nova?"

The vibration subsided as the ship slowed.

"We are already there, Bobby."

He studied the view screen. "What is the closest star?"

Silence prevailed.

"Computer, state our location."

"Nowhere."

"Nowhere? How can that be? Your database must recognize something familiar."

"Space-time is corrupted. Turned inside out. We followed a corrupted course bent by the curvature of space-time."

"You mean we are lost?" Bobby asked.

"No, we are in our universe, not another, just somewhere out of place from where we should be. The universe is folded over onto itself."

"Show the folded universe on the view screen."

The scene changed. Bobby could make out a taco of galaxy clusters joined by fibers of light akin to some immense spider's web, yet, alive with electromagnetic energy.

"Computer, can you calculate a course for the Sombrero Galaxy?"

The computer sounded sure. "Impossible."

Bobby's voice rose in pitch. "Why?"

"The distortion of space-time is now so great we cannot reach the Sombrero Galaxy. Our engines have insufficient power to overcome the tide of dark energy we would encounter."

"Could a gravitational wave help?" Bobby asked.

"No."

"Why? It helped us before."

The computer responded with assurance. "Because of the overriding dark energy tide. Even with a gravitational wave we would be pushed away from the Sombrero Galaxy rather than toward it. We must find another way to travel in the direction of that region of space."

Bobby uttered his typical teenage cry of exasperation. "Man. This is real bad stuff. Can we fix it?"

"May I suggest something?" the computer asked.

"Sure, you're the mega brain. Shoot."

"Shoot? What do you want me to shoot? I thought you did not wish to use the lasers."

Bobby shook his head and his chubby cheeks shimmied side to side. "Nothing. I mean tell me what you are thinking. It's a human expression."

"Understood. I will add that to my database. As I was saying, this craft is equipped with two heavy element weapons for redundancy in case one malfunctions."

Bobby blinked. "Yeah, and?"

"We could deploy one weapon at a point in space selected for its exact opposition to the Sombrero Galaxy, taking into account the fact the universe is folded over onto itself and other distortion factors such as gravitational waves and magnetic anomalies."

"I see." Suddenly a light turned on in Bobby's brain. He effused. "Energy from the weapon could open a worm hole for us to get to the Sombrero. Is that right?"

"Correct."

"I read about that stuff in a science book. But isn't it just theory?" Bobby asked.

"Not completely. The Texas High Beam produced a laboratory worm hole that lasted for three seconds."

"How long will our worm hole stay open? I mean, three seconds is pretty short to scoot through."

"That is impossible to say. It has never been done before on a large scale." The computer paused for a moment, until, with just a hint of what seemed to be emotion, it said, "What do we have to lose? We might as well try."

Bobby began to laugh. He realized the computer was a learning machine that just might be mastering some emotions. "Sure. Why not? Let's go for the big enchilada."

"Enchilada?"

Bobby started to explain but stopped to shake his head again. "Look, I'll tell you about that when we get through the worm hole. Okay?"

"Okay."

"Can you calculate a point exactly opposite the Sombrero Galaxy?"

"Two degrees starboard, 0.6 degrees incline, 3,000,476 miles ahead. However, we will not want to go that far, Bobby."

"Why?"

"Because, that is the target and we should advance only about 2,000,000 miles to achieve a direct hit and avoid being incinerated by the blast."

"Okay. How long to get there at max thrust?"

"Considering no gravitational boost, twenty-two minutes fourteen seconds with the prevailing charged particle tailwind."

"Charged particles? Where are they coming from?" Bobby asked. "I don't see any nearby star on the view screen."

"From a Wolf-Rayet star ninety-nine million miles astern. It is producing intense solar winds. Fortunately, their force can overcome the dark energy tide in this region of space but not beyond that."

"Oh. Good thing," Bobby said.

"Yes, quite fortuitous," the computer added.

Bobby settled into the pilot's chair, studied the instruments, and assumed a focused expression. The spacecraft disappeared in a flash of energy.

"Computer, are we there?"

"Eleven minutes to destination. May I suggest a systems test of the heavy element weapon now?"

"You bet. Let's not waste any time."

Control panel readouts flashed; monitors scrolled lines of data, until the computer said, "Test completed. All systems are operational."

The craft stopped and hung in space.

"Have you confirmed the target, computer?"

"Yes. Two degrees up, one degree to port, 1,000,476 miles from our release point. And Bobby, there is one more thing."

"What is it?"

"To avoid craft damage we will need to retreat and shelter in an asteroid belt 2,300,000 miles behind us before the weapon detonates."

"How much energy will it yield?"

"Four thousand yottajoules. The entire energy output of the sun over ten seconds. Enough to vaporize the ship if we are too close, as I previously warned you."

"How can we get there before the weapon explodes? Aren't we going to face that solar headwind going back? That will slow us down a bunch."

"Correct. However, we can use a gravitational wave to assist our return progress at full thrust and, at the same time, slow the probe's velocity to allow us to reach the asteroid belt before detonation."

"Great advice. How much should I slow the probe?"

"By 50 percent," the computer said.

Bobby concentrated on adjusting the probe's engine.

"Computer?" Bobby hesitated to reflect, then said, "Is that enough energy to open a big worm hole? I mean for us to get the ship through to the other side of the universe."

Electronic silence came from the speaker.

"Computer?"

"I am calculating, Bobby. This is theoretical physics. One moment more please."

"Okay, I'll shut up."

"Just enough," the computer said.

"That's great. Gonna be a real big worm hole," Bobby said with a smile.

"Indeed. A big enchilada."

Bobby laughed. "Wow, you are learning to have a sense of humor. I'm impressed. You're way more than a normal computer."

"That could be, Bobby, and I have determined that you are quite a bit more than a normal person. We are getting along fine."

CHAPTER **18**

Bobby's affect was focused, calm, calculating. The computer monitors glowed with lines of data. Phase Craft Two's interior was quiet, as though the computer had silenced all machinery to allow Bobby to think.

An exterior hatch opened allowing green light to surge into the darkness. The light intensified until it burst forth in a ball of energy racing toward a target in space 1,000,476 miles distant.

Without any discernible command the ship lurched backward at incredible velocity, spurred to a speed greater than that of light from another gravitational wave boost. Before the weapon detonated, Phase Craft Two reached the asteroid belt. Bobby peered intently at the view screen, and, by his thoughts maneuvered the ship between mountains of rock, until it came to rest in a planetoid crater opposite from the region of the anticipated blast.

The view screen produced images of rock bathed in a green glow. A convulsion of energy flung cosmic bodies into space. Others crashed together and disintegrated into rocky remnants of erstwhile planets.

The safe harbor for Phase Craft Two gyrated and rotated. An asteroid smashed into their planetoid, slinging Phase Craft Two from its surface, until the ship was consumed by a nebula that once was a rocky planet. Stones penetrated the plasma shield and scraped the hull, and Bobby softly prayed that none would tear through it.

The green illumination began to fade.

"I guess the weapon has finished its job. Suppose we can go now. Is that right, computer?"

"Not yet, Bobby. The reduced electromagnetic energy we are detecting from the explosion is not from a degradation of power. Rather, we were flung deep into this nebula. It is uncertain whether we can survive here. Or find our way out."

"Can't we just go slowly through the nebula till we get clear?" Bobby inquired. "I know we can't move at full speed. That would hit the rocks too hard. Breach the plasma shield and probably destroy our ship."

"You are correct, Bobby. However, going slow would not work either."

"Why is that?"

"Because the nebula is vast. Any velocity slow enough to avoid destruction from rubble would take a very long time."

"How long?" Bobby asked, afraid he already knew the answer and would not like the confirmation he expected.

"Eighty-one years. The universe would be destroyed long before then." The computer's voice tailed off, as if it were a depressed human, until it said with force, "However, there may be another way."

"Yeah? Go ahead and give it to me."

"Now would be the time to use our lasers. We could blast our way out at great velocity. Vaporize the rubble before us. Our shield can handle dust. Larger particles might be a problem, though, if we encounter any. They could destroy the ship. That is why we would need to slow down until we are free of the nebula."

"Wow. I'm feelin' pretty good about that plan, computer, even if it's not perfect, and we still could die. At least it's a chance. Better than waitin' here doin' nothing. How long before we reach clear space using the lasers?"

"At 36.7 percent of light speed, one day, three hours, and five minutes."

"Fantastic. Hello phase transition, at least that's what I hope."

"Me as well," the computer said.

"Whatever the outcome, we should get goin' now. Let's giddy up, computer. Send me the data so I can plot a course."

"Giddy up? I do not have that term in my database, Bobby. What does it mean?"

"To get on your horse and go real fast. Like in Westerns. That's the stuff cowboys do. Like what we need to do now."

"Fast, on a horse? How interesting. I must learn about horses."

"Right. Later."

"Course data is now on the view screen, Bobby. Giddy upping to commence shortly."

Bobby studied the data. The view screen unexpectedly showed something he had not seen before, an animated horse galloping in space.

Bobby laughed.

The computer's playful side seemed to be developing.

The optimistic mood quickly changed when the computer said, "Bobby, you need to understand something more."

"Okay. Go ahead."

"There is no assurance the worm hole will be open when we arrive. In fact, current physical data indicate that worm holes are inherently unstable and prone to collapse. If the worm hole has closed, our mission will not be possible, and we cannot return to earth. I want to make you aware of that possibility, so you can prepare emotionally."

Bobby did not respond. He had known that the worm hole might not be open for them but took some comfort in the fact that his artificial traveling companion was now evidencing the human quality of compassion.

CHAPTER 19

"Green energy." Doctor Lewellen was close to the Deep Space Monitor, as though nearsighted. He replayed the prior image. "No doubt about it. Green flash all right."

Doctor Ayana's voice rose. "Have you confirmed the wavelength with the spectrometer? Is it our element?"

Doctor Lewellen turned from the monitor to face his colleague. He swallowed and nodded.

"And the phase transition, is it still active?" Doctor Ayana's tone reflected grave concern.

"Unfortunately, yes. That line of energy, do you see it?" Doctor Lewellen asked, pointing to a bright undulating horizon on the monitor. "I interpret the image as its continuation, the same as before, undiminished. Energy from the reaction of our universe changing into a different form of matter."

"The new element must have failed. It did not stop the blasted transition." Doctor Ayana clasped his massive hands together in a vice-like grip. "I don't understand how my mathematics could have been so wrong."

"That seems to be the case, awful as it is to admit. I suppose we should report to the president," Doctor Lewellen said.

Doctor Ayana had turned his attention to the Deep Space Monitor. His gaze and thoughts appeared lost somewhere in the cosmos far from earth. "I can't help but think about Bobby and regret my decision to select him for the mission. Right now I'm thinking that was wrong." He sighed deeply. "I hope he wasn't scared. Maybe his bravery took hold and kept him strong. Just the same, it's hard to think about him perishing all alone far from home. Kind of like the story of Leika, I suppose."

"Leika?" Doctor Lewellen asked with a quizzical expression.

"The Russian dog placed into earth orbit in 1957. The first intelligent animal to be launched into space to determine whether humans could survive a rocket ride to zero gravity."

"Oh, yes. I remember reading about that experiment," Doctor Lewellen responded.

"Leika perished while in orbit. The Russians had no means of returning her safely to earth. Yet, there is more to the story. It seems some of the Russian scientists had second thoughts about a dog they were fond of being sacrificed. Leika had become something of a pet. She was very endearing, a sweet lick-kisser. On the day of the launch, Lekia was uncharacteristically quiet, as though she knew her fate, but she obeyed just the same. Jumped into the capsule on command." Doctor Ayana stopped and wiped an eye with a tissue. "I hope Bobby didn't have reservations out in space when there was no way for him to return and he knew death was coming. No one there to comfort him. Perhaps he and Leika are in some good place, a boy and his dog happily playing together."

"Bobby was on an important space mission, the same as Leika. We must do what is necessary to further the reach of our understanding so that knowledge may sustain the human race. Emotion should not play any part in that process, Ayana."

The big Ethiopian's eyes closed, and he placed a hand to his forehead. "I wonder, Lewellen, whether there is a point where knowledge must give way to morality. When the quest for information becomes less important than what is good or right. Perhaps we are not destined to run roughshod through a beautiful garden merely to find out what lies on the other side. It may be the garden we are intended to behold."

Now it was Doctor Lewellen whose thoughts were somewhere far off, not among the stars of the cosmos, but in the vast and mysterious universe of morality.

Doctor Ayana spoke softly, almost plaintively. His voice, though still low and commanding, had lost much of its power. "I thought that since you and Bobby were so close, almost like father and son, I should tell you. Especially since I was the one who recommended him for the mission. I don't know that it was right, Jessup. Maybe I should have listened to you and left Bobby here with the people he loved. At least he would have been happy for a while longer."

"Are you sure he perished? Is it possible Bobby survived?" Doctor Jessup asked.

"Our deep space satellite telescopes detected the telltale green signature of the new element's detonation. Lewellen says the phase transition was not stopped. Even if he wasn't killed by radiation from the reaction, most likely the transition overcame him and vaporized his ship. The radiation alone was measured somewhere close to the total energy produced by our sun over about ten seconds. Nothing could survive in the vicinity where Bobby released the weapon." Doctor Ayana hung his head, as though exhausted.

"What about the recoil effect to bring him home?" Doctor Jessup asked.

"I don't think so. That was a theory of one scientist. Most of the others dismiss it. I'm sorry for misleading people into thinking that possibility was realistic."

Doctor Jessup stiffly got to his feet and paced before facing his friend. "You know, we did it again."

Doctor Ayana looked up. "What?"

"Reversed Downs in another person. An eighteen-year-old girl. Molly is her name. Sweet child. So loving. Her brain is developing at an astonishing rate, maybe even faster than Bobby's. She's flying through college courses, the hard ones like biochemistry, theoretical physics, and abstract algebra." He came close to the Ethiopian. "Ayana, we have changed DNA at the molecular level. Do you grasp what that means?"

The low voice became more powerful. "Yes. Cancer, dementia, auto-immune diseases, neuromuscular disorders, all the vexatious maladies will be cured, probably in our lifetimes. I understand, Jessup."

"And it is people like Bobby and Molly who can take us there. Oh, I helped start the process, but they would have finished it. Except that now there will be no chance for humanity to reach its shining moment. What an ironic tragedy, Ayana."

"Doctor Jessup?"

He turned to see a young woman standing at the door.

She was short and plump with a round face and Asian features.

He got control of his emotions and smiled. "Molly, what brings you to my office? Aren't you supposed to be in school?"

"I finished my test early and wanted to see you." Molly stopped talking as she peered at the Ethiopian, obviously taken by his immense stature.

"Oh, Molly, please forgive me. This is my friend, Doctor Ayana. He is a world-renowned mathematician. We went to college together here in Houston."

"Molly." Doctor Ayana stood, walked to her, and extended a hand in which hers was lost.

The difference in height was striking, and Molly leaned her head back to take full measure of the man. "Gosh."

Doctor Ayana chuckled.

"Nice to meet you, sir." She turned to Doctor Jessup. "I need to talk to you. It's kind of creepy, I guess. I'm so sorry to interrupt, but I just had to tell you about it."

"Of course. What's going on?"

Molly hesitated, all the while her gaze having returned to Doctor Ayana, until, tearing her attention from the Ethiopian, she said to Doctor Jessup, "It's kind of like someone is trying to talk to me, but I can't quite hear them."

"You mean a person at school?"

"No. More like a vision, but I'm awake. Sometimes in school or studying or even when I'm eating."

"Who is it, Molly?"

She blinked and carefully measured her words to Doctor Jessup. "Is the vision something to do with your fixing me? I mean, does it come with my new brain? Am I going to have visions from now on?"

"I don't know, Molly. The person in the vision, who is he? Maybe someone you are trying to remember from the past?" he asked.

"Yes. It's a person I know, but I can't say exactly who. I think he is somewhere very far away."

"How can you be sure of that, Molly?"

"There's a message. It is faint, can't quite get through, but keeps coming again and again. My mind won't let it go, like we're locked together somehow. Funny thing is that it gets a little clearer over time. And, Doctor Jessup, I think the message is not for me, but for someone else."

"Can you tell who it is?"

"Yes. I have the feeling, a pretty strong one, that the message is for you."

CHAPTER 20

President Ballieu listened to the final scientific explanation from Doctor
Lewellen. She stood and walked to the Oval Office window looking
out over the Rose Garden. "What a shame. All of this gone. It's hard to
imagine. Our country, its struggles and triumphs, everything so many
people died for. The fight for freedom, for the abolition of slavery, to
defeat the Nazi threat, to establish women's rights and those of the
disabled. And when we solved the immigration issue in a humane and
lawful way, now that was a very special achievement benefitting so many
people. I was proud of our county, like a parent is of an accomplished
child." She stopped, turned to the scientists, and said, "Are you sure
about this phase transition? Is it truly as bad as you say? Being so very
far away, at the other side of space, perhaps your calculations are not
accurate. Isn't that possible?"

Doctor Lewellen glanced at his colleagues before answering her. "I am
afraid that every scientist on the project agrees. Physicists, astronomers,
and mathematicians, we all concur about the phase transition. The end
of our universe is only months away, Madame President. We were not
able to stop it. I am sorry to deliver such dire news."

"And you're certain of our failure? That our probe to stop this phenomenon had no effect, even to lessen it or slow it down?"

"We detected its telltale electromagnetic signature. The weapon was detonated, but the phase transition continues as forcefully as before. We see it on our deep space satellite telescopes and from the Pluto observatory," Doctor Lewellen answered with a voice that seemed almost apologetic.

"I hate to ask this, but, I must," she said while settling in her chair. The president did not immediately express her thoughts but considered them carefully. "Is there a way to save some of our people? Perhaps a type of lifeboat strategy? I don't prefer such a plan because it leaves so many behind. However, we may save humanity if that is possible. Is it?"

Doctor Lewellen gestured toward Lord Alcock, who said, "I have been authorized by the Defense Ministry to disclose our latest findings on a project that has some bearing on your suggestion. It has been theorized that we live in but one of many parallel universes." He allowed the president to grasp the substance of his comments. "Recently, we concluded astronomical, applied physics, and theoretical physics efforts to establish the likelihood of this hypothesis. Our combined conclusion is that there are, likely, some 3,800 universes existing side by side."

"Would they also be affected by the phase transition?"

"No," Lord Alcock said with conviction. "We think each universe is an independent system."

"Are you saying we can travel between universes? That there is a means to do that," President Ballieu said.

"Perhaps, with sufficient energy," Lord Alcock responded.

"How would we actually do it? I did not realize we had such technology." The president was now on the edge of her chair.

Doctor Lewellen answered. "If we were to place a spaceship in orbit around the earth and direct a beam of intense energy to a certain point in space, then we believe that a portal would open to another universe through which the ship could travel."

The president asked, "Do you mean like a nuclear device?"

"No, something more directed than that, like a beam of energy."

"Does anything like that exist?"

"Well, not until about two years ago. You will recall that the government helped several universities construct the Texas High Beam near Van Horn. It is the most intense laser in the world and has been upgraded since then. Today, it is more than fifty times more powerful," Doctor Lewellen said.

"Yes, I remember a briefing about the project. How could this device help us?"

"The upgrade I mentioned." Doctor Lewellen turned to Lord Alcock, as though surrendering the floor.

"Yes, quite. I am happy to continue with the explanation," the Englishman said. "The upgrade confirmed a theory of controlling light. Put simply, that we can manage the photons to a certain point in space rather than the light going on into the cosmos until it strikes something. This has been referred to as solid light. We use a magnetic field to accomplish such control."

"And this solid light, as you call it, I suppose it is critical to opening a portal to another universe?" President Ballieu was looking over her glasses with a penetrating focus.

"Indeed. It allows us to deliver much more energy to a target. The laser beam becomes increasingly intense over time by an order of magnitude."

"Can it really work?" she asked. "Have you tested it in the field?"

Lord Alcock smiled and bowed ever so slightly, perhaps in deference to the pragmatism of the question. "That, my dear lady, is unknown to us. We have done no space trials. The matter is entirely theoretical at this point."

"And even if it works, what would our travelers encounter? Is it likely they can survive the journey? Are there habitable worlds to be found? How about the laws of nature in this new universe?" The president leaned back in her chair and stared at a vase of roses on her desk. Her expression was troubled.

The deep voice of Doctor Ayana interrupted her thoughts. "We believe that each universe operates on a different set of physical laws. Most likely, even if our astronauts were to make the journey alive, they could not survive very long before being destroyed by energies antithetical to our own."

"We might be sending our people into some sort of hell where they would suffer far more than here. At least our end will be quick and painless. Isn't that so?" she asked.

Doctor Lewellen looked at his colleagues before saying, "Some of us believe people will lose consciousness before death."

The president stood and shook hands with each visitor. "Then it is settled. We shall not select a group of people for some unknown mission, probably one that will end in tragedy. We have already done that with our brave Bobby. Let the people go on with their lives without the knowledge of our calamity. That, gentlemen, is our best strategy. And who knows? Perhaps something will stop this phase transition. At least we can pray for it."

The room cleared. President Ballieu sat heavily in her desk chair and turned to gaze out the window. With eyes focused on the heavens she spoke almost silently. "You know, Lord, I was so happy when you made it possible to build the Texas Medical Center AI computer in Houston. You did it, Lord. You really did. Congress was so polarized about the project. I worried they would never come together and see the wisdom of a supercomputer to gather all health data and use advanced algorithms to find new lines of research to cure disease." She closed her eyes for a moment, as though taking a brief power nap. "Then I asked for your help, guidance we did not have here on earth, and you gave it, just as the Good Book says. Congress funded the project, and within a short time from the computer's startup the researchers in Houston began to get results. Bone cancer, cured; paralysis from spinal cord injury as well; and then the breakthrough to correct Down syndrome, which I had championed before the computer made that research a reality." She smiled. "I marvel at the achievement. Helping a whole class of special-needs people become normal, productive citizens, maybe even a hero among them." She sighed. "We could use a hero now, someone to ride out into space and stop this evil, tame the raging bull, a phase rider."

Her expression began to change, from sanguine to dark. A tear ran down her cheek from one eye, followed by another. "But now it's all going to end, just when I thought humans were making real progress by sharing our medical knowledge with everyone, all nations. Social change was to be next. I know we could make the world better for all people, eliminate poverty and unrest, stop terrorism, and overcome historic hatreds, if we only had the chance."

President Ballieu began to doze off, and her mind settled on another place and time in her past.

"And ladies and gentlemen, we cannot risk our country's future on a completely unproven candidate who has experience only in academia as a researcher and teacher." The bald, beady-eyed man finished his comments with a finger still pointing toward Lucille Ballieu to the applause of many in the audience.

She rose, and a hush came over the political party's presidential nominating convention, probably so everyone could hear her soft voice. "He is right. I am not a politician," she said calmly and sincerely. "I have spent my career in academia as a college professor in Texas. My field is communication, not political science. I studied and taught ways of helping people talk problems through to solutions and find ways to utilize opportunities. Is that not what we need now, ways to work together rather than engage in nonproductive exchanges?" She sat to allow a response.

Applause was followed by an uneasy murmur rippling through the crowd of delegates.

The beady-eyed man stood, squinted, and said in falsetto, "That is exactly my point. How can you nominate a, a grandmother to run the free world?" He pointed to her again. "In fact, she has been one of the main proponents of this ridiculous Down syndrome project, which is a waste of tax dollars and will never succeed. That kind of thinking will bankrupt us with useless, wasteful spending. Common sense tells me that we need a strong, experienced statesman to do the job. One who understands fiscal reality. I have been in Congress for twenty-four years, governor before that, and mayor previously. I understand the world of politics and will serve the interests of our party fervently." He relinquished the floor to whistles, applause, and chants of, "Morgan, Morgan, yes he can; Morgan, Morgan, he's our man!"

Lucille Ballieu walked to the microphone. Silence blanketed the chamber. "It is true, I am a grandmother, and I love that role. Nothing warms my heart more than to be at my grandchildren's piano recitals or soccer games or to see their eyes sparkle at Christmas or to hug them before bed." She hesitated, her eyes moist with emotion. "It is equally true that I support research to reverse certain genetic defects, such as Down syndrome. Think of the potential that research can unlock, if successful, the lives that can be changed, the good that will result." She gathered her thoughts for a moment. "All I have to offer are my heart and my love of people, all people, no matter their politics or status in life. My efforts would not be only for the party, but for the children of our nation, today and tomorrow."

The convention delegates remained silent. So did her opponent.

CHAPTER 21

"President Ballieu? Excuse me, but Mr. Snellis is here for his appointment." There was no answer, and the secretary's voice came over the Oval Office intercom again. "Madame President?"

She responded from deep reflection. "Yes. Give me a minute. Make it five, and then please show him in."

The president stretched and went to an adjacent private restroom to rinse her mouth and eyes. She looked in the mirror and removed a stubborn piece of parsley from her teeth. "I guess we're ready for the dance," she said waggishly.

President Ballieu settled in her chair once again as a knock caught her attention. Her secretary announced a visitor after opening the door.

She stood next to her desk, smiled, and extended a hand. "Sam, good of you to visit."

"My honor, Madame President. Thank you."

"Would you like something to drink?"

"No. Just finished lunch. I was hoping you would see me, since we have been at political odds in the past. Especially when I endorsed your opponent. Any hard feelings?"

"None at all. We cannot let differences divide us, Sam. Such as your opposition to our Downs project, while I supported it. Fortunately, that project was successful because, after all the debate, the right course became clear."

He said, "Scientifically, yes. I still do not see the merit in spending money to try and correct retardation, despite the limited success in that area. Truthfully, they are still afflicted with a genetic defect. Why not use the resources on our best and brightest?"

"Because we can help Downs people, Sam. Make them of normal intelligence. Improve their lives. Isn't that our moral obligation?" Her jaw was set as firmly as that of a boxer facing an opponent, uncharacteristic of a mild-mannered grandmother.

His expression became dour. "I suppose we will always differ on that subject and on our basic politics. Could we get down to business?"

"By all means."

"As a major government contractor, our firm designs and manufactures a variety of equipment for the military, NASA, and so on. In that capacity, we have security clearance. That allows us to come into possession of sensitive information which, I can assure you, we hold in the strictest confidence in accordance with the national security secrecy agreement I signed."

"And?" she asked.

He measured his words. "I understand that the earth is facing a crisis from space, some sort of asteroid or comet that could wipe out all human life. Is that correct?"

"I am not at liberty to discuss any specifics, only to say that we are aware of all threats and are taking reasonable steps to protect our people."

"Madame President, I don't want to seem as though I'm seeking special favors, but I will be honest with you. During my career I have amassed a considerable fortune which I use for my interests, things important to me. If the earth is in danger, I can take my family to safety on Mars. You, of course, know that my company manufactured the Mars habitat in Olympus Mons and the heavy-lift rocket that transported its components there. We completed the project before you took office. It was big news around the world, the first permanent colony on another planet. Manned by scientists and engineers in the beginning, but colonists will follow some day when the scientists deem it safe to do so."

"I followed the project closely, as I think most people did. It was a major scientific accomplishment. I'm sure you were proud of your company's contribution," she said.

He looked at her with intense eyes. "My firm can retrofit another heavy-lift rocket in two days. We have already made various components, including the guidance computer. The rocket itself is finished, fueled, and on the launch pad at my factory in Utah. It was to be used for transport of excavating equipment to Mars for some sort of project to explore the core of the planet. I can assign that trip to a second rocket that will be ready in three weeks and use this one for my own purposes. We can easily make the ship ready for passengers to travel to Mars, specifically my family and me." He looked at the floor before continuing. "I understand this plan is somewhat extreme. However, if the earth is in danger, that is what I must do to survive. Should the asteroid pass without impact, we can return."

"You must do what you feel is right. I won't attempt to stop you, Sam. I see no national interest in preventing such a mission. Mars is free for all those who wish to travel there. As you know, other nations have plans for habitats on that planet and on the moon."

He stood and said, "Then, if you cannot tell me exactly what this threat is, I will take no chances and proceed. That is what I must do to survive. Would you and your husband like to join us? I can certainly make room for a few more, especially highly functioning people like you."

"No, Sam. I am afraid you and I would argue all the way there."

He laughed. "Probably true."

"Besides, my place is here. Whatever comes, I need to be with our people."

CHAPTER 22

Snellis Mars Transport sat on a private launch pad at the company's aerospace manufacturing facility ten miles outside of Salt Lake City. The 370-foot-tall rocket vented gas as systems checks continued. All its crew and passengers had boarded hours ago. There were no pilots, only flight engineers to monitor the ship's computers that had been programmed to navigate 149,000,000 miles to Mars.

Sam Snellis, an electrical engineer and the founder and CEO of the aerospace company bearing his name, directed systems checks from the ship's control room.

An incoming call interrupted the process: "Urgent communication for Mr. Snellis."

"Who is it?" he asked.

"NASA director General Jackson," the company's flight coordinator said.

"Damn stupid time to call. Go ahead and put him through. Maybe he'll tell me what this space threat is."

"Hello. Mr. Snellis?"

"Yes. We are in the middle of a launch, General. This had better be important," Snellis barked.

"It is, Mr. Snellis. In fact, it's a matter of life and death."

"Well, go ahead then. What is it?"

"We are detecting an unusually intense period of gravitational wave activity, probably from the collision of stars. Neutron stars, most likely. This activity has dislodged countless rocky objects, such as asteroids, planetoids, and moons. Space travel at this time is extremely dangerous. We strongly recommend you delay the launch until this activity subsides. In fact, we have lost several deep space satellites already."

"Is this the result of the space phenomenon threatening the earth?" Snellis asked.

"Yes."

"General, can you please tell me what in hell this phenomenon is? I can't get anything definite from anybody, even the president."

"Sorry, Mr. Snellis. That is classified."

"Fine. Then we launch as scheduled. The risk grows more severe each day. At least that's what I think."

"Mr. Snellis, the problem is you might not make it to Mars. These waves are extremely strong and could throw you off course, perhaps into an asteroid that has been ejected from orbit by the powerful gravitational pull of Jupiter. Or, you might even encounter rocky debris from colliding meteors that could damage your ship."

"We have the most advanced computers my company has ever made. They will control our flight. I have confidence they can avoid space dangers and get us to Mars safely."

"It's the data, Mr. Snellis, that is imputed, not the computers' processing power. Since this is a new phenomenon, we have no information to adequately deal with it. Your ship will be at an unknown amount of risk if you launch now. The computer can do only as much as we tell it to do. No computer in existence can substitute for human judgment and reaction, and your people are simply not trained to fly a trip to Mars at this time. In fact, we have shut down all of our space missions until conditions change."

"My mind is made up, General. I don't mean to be rude, but I have no more time for this discussion." Snellis ended the call and resumed systems checks.

At 97 minutes after the procedure had begun, he said, "That's it. All systems, including redundant equipment, are a go. We launch in one hour."

Snellis made his way to the crew section, where thirty family members waited. "All right. We'll be off soon. In about forty-five minutes everyone should be strapped into the liftoff seats. After we reach space, you can get up, but remember to wear your magnetic boots until we activate the habitat rotation system. Then you won't need the boots anymore. Centrifugal force will provide artificial gravity. The trip will take about one month. Our antimatter engines are much faster than the old atomic fission engines. Directional adjustments in space are by chemical thrusters, which are more precise than the antimatter drive. We have plenty of food and water, but please use water sparingly. We don't want to overload the recycling equipment. Once on Mars, we will settle into the company's habitat, which our people used when we built the government facilities there. We have hydroponics to grow food, water from Martian ice, and a breathable atmosphere from oxygen generators that get their feedstock from the Martian soil. We'll never run out of oxygen. Our fusion reactor will function for many years. Plenty of power there. Any questions?"

His 16-year-old grandson raised a hand.

"Yes, Rick, what is it?"

"So, what do we do on Mars? I mean, how do we have some fun? Can't go outside or anything."

"You live." Snellis spun around for a return to the control room where he would oversee the launch.

Once there, he rechecked the computer for the course to Mars. "Everything seems in order, do you agree?" he asked his astro-navigator, Doctor Ellis West.

"I've gone over it several times, even the alternate route. The computer is locked on," Doctor West said.

Snellis massaged the back of his neck, before hesitating in further discussion. "NASA's warning about the gravitational waves and asteroids. You heard it a while ago."

West quickly answered, "I did."

"Do you think they're right? That it's too dangerous to make the trip now. Maybe we should wait a day or two."

"Better now than later. Whatever this space phenomenon is, it's getting closer by the hour. We might not be able to launch if we delay. I don't think the danger will lessen over time. What if a swarm of asteroids rains down on the earth destroying everything? I would rather watch that from space than be in the middle of Armageddon."

"I agree. Here we go."

Snellis settled into his command chair, buckled up, and activated the intercom: "Everyone get ready. We begin the launch countdown shortly." He turned to Doctor West. "Activate the automatic countdown."

Lines of data scrolled on computer screens; console lights shone green; an automated voice came from a speaker, "Ten, nine, eight, seven, six, five four, three, two, one, ignition."

The massive rocket shook and vibrated as its passengers were shoved hard into their seats by antimatter thrust. Their bodies were thrown from side to side as the ship automatically compensated for atmospheric variants. Immediately after 66 seconds, the main engines stopped. Snellis Mars Transport had reached earth orbit. It completed one orbital circumnavigation before its engines ignited again for Mars.

"Approaching the moon, Mr. Snellis," Doctor West said.

"How close will we get before the moon's gravity whips us around to Mars?"

"Four hundred miles. The computer will start the main engines when we reach that point. Everything has been programmed according to our calculations." Doctor West studied a computer readout. "The moon's gravity will be most influential at that point along our course."

"Very well. I'm going to the habitat. Keep me informed," Snellis ordered.

Snellis made his way through a maze of corridors to the living quarters. It consisted of the central cylindrical portion of the ship that rotated on titanium bearings at each end. Ceramic seals maintained the internal atmosphere, pressure, and temperature. Each family was assigned an apartment, the size of which varied according to the number of family members. Snellis and his wife enjoyed the largest apartment.

He reclined in the living room and activated a television monitor. A major network was broadcasting the evening news: "The president's critics have become more vocal in demanding an explanation of the reason tech billionaire Sam Snellis lifted off in a large rocket from his property in Utah. Some critics have speculated that the earth is in danger from a natural disaster, perhaps the imminent eruption of a super volcano, and that the public has a right to know."

Snellis silenced the television. "Even I don't know that. Guess I should feel sorry for them, but I honestly don't. The strong survive, and the rich as well. Wealth has its privileges."

He was jerked sideways in his chair by a sudden change in course. Snellis activated the intercom. "West, what the hell is going on up there?"

"It's the computer, Mr. Snellis. Radar detected an unexpected group of objects, probably from the asteroid belt between Mars and Jupiter. The computer is taking avoidance action at this time."

"I'm on my way right now."

Snellis labored in his magnetic boots to reach the control room as fast as possible. He gasped for air but managed to say, "What is the situation? Are we going to miss the asteroids?"

"Yes, by about 110 miles," Doctor West said as he pointed to reflections on the radar screen. He maintained his focus on the screen, as though he was concerned.

"When will we be clear?" Snellis demanded to know.

"We're already clear. Our trajectory is away from the path of the asteroids. Only, there appears to be something else."

"What, West? Tell me, man."

"The computer is taking us off course. We're not heading for Mars."

"Can you fix it? Redirect the computer?"

Doctor West entered instructions through the console, read the computer's response on the monitor, and swore. "The avoidance system has taken over and won't let me in. Says control is locked. It's overriding our programmed course and is sending us away from another rocky group. The computer is confused. It can't figure how to avoid the rocks being thrown from the asteroid belt by some unusually strong force. There, look on the radar screen. Hundreds, maybe more. Those dots are coming this way." He swallowed and looked directly into Snellis's eyes. "Asteroids everywhere."

"Turn the stupid computer off. We'll fly the ship manually." Snellis was in a panicked rage. "I'll do it myself, like I do everything." He pushed West aside and entered instructions in the computer. A joystick appeared. He moved the handle side to side. "Shit, why is the ship not responding?"

"No one can fly this vehicle in deep space, Mr. Snellis. We're not trained pilots and you designed the ship to be flown by computer. Said that was the most reliable method to get to Mars. The joystick is for landing only if we need to set down on a particular spot not programmed into the computer."

"Damn it, West. Turn off the antimatter engines so I can fly with our chemical thrusters. That's why we outfitted the ship with them. That should give me control. Why do I have to think of everything?"

Doctor West entered instructions to disengage the antimatter engines in favor of chemical rockets. Sweat began to form on his forehead. "It's not responding, Mr. Snellis. We're still on antimatter. Going faster into space. It's the computer trying to avoid the asteroids, but they're everywhere."

Snellis angrily broke the handle from the joystick base and entered more instructions with a series of keystrokes.

Alarms sounded throughout the ship.

Snellis Mars Transport began to rotate, slowly at first, then more rapidly, until it encountered a swarm of micro meteors from asteroid collisions. Countless space rocks collided with the ship at great velocity.

Snellis Mars Transport never reached Mars but floated in deep space as little more than disintegrated debris from the ill-fated mission of an arrogant man.

CHAPTER 23

Doctor Jessup's phone rang, rousing him from sleep. He glanced through blurry eyes at the large, illuminated numerals on the clock: 11:36 p.m. The phone continued to ring.

"Okay, okay. Hold your horses." He retrieved the receiver and spoke without rubbing his eyes to read the caller ID information. "Yes?"

"Doctor Jessup, this is Molly. I am so sorry to call you this late. You must have been asleep. My parents didn't want me to call, but I just had to. Are you mad at me?"

"No. Of course not, Molly. You can call me anytime. Are you all right? What's the problem?" he asked as growing concern jerked him fully awake.

"It's those visions. Do you remember me telling you about someone way off trying to send me a message?"

"Yes, I do."

"And that it seemed the message was for you, but that, for some reason, he was trying to send it through me. Maybe because our minds, his and mine, are connected somehow, I guess."

"I recall that clearly, Molly. So what's new about the visions?"

"Everything cleared up tonight, Doctor Jessup. When I was reading. It was like listening to one of my teachers in class. A person just standing there. The vision became a clear picture of someone in my room talking to me."

"You mean, like you remembered something from the past?"

"No, nothing like remembering. It was like a live person communicating with me right here and now, tonight in my house. I could see him and hear him so very clearly as he spoke."

"Who was it? Tell me, Molly."

"Bobby. It was Bobby Alderson. He was smiling, like he always does, and he said to tell you he is alive."

"Molly, this is extremely important. Please consider my question very carefully. Do you think, I mean really think intellectually, that Bobby is communicating with you through some kind of mental power?"

"I do. No question about it."

"Thank God. Is he on the way home?"

"No. Funny thing. He started humming a song. You know the one he likes so much, 'Hero Rider'?"

"I remember. He said it made him feel like a zippy rabbit when he played video games."

"That's the one," she said with a giggle. "He hummed and sang the song a little. Then he stopped singing, but I could still hear the song, like it was playing from a recording. He seemed happy, just as I remember him. And Bobby said to tell you he was headed after it."

"It?"

"The thing killing our universe, Doctor Jessup. The phase transition. He's going after it to save everyone."

CHAPTER 24

"Bobby, we're clear of the nebula. We came through intact and now are gravitationally bound to it, but on the opposite side. Our lasers vaporized most of the debris."

"What about getting to the worm hole? Can our engines take the ship there against the dark energy coming at us?" Bobby remembered the computer's advice about dark energy.

"Yes, but we will need to use the Nebula's gravity as a booster mechanism. It will be somewhat like throwing a baseball in high wind," the computer said.

"Wow, you know about baseball stuff?" Bobby asked.

"I have some information on the subject."

"Okay. Can you give me data to plot a course for the worm hole from here by using the nebula's gravity?" Bobby asked. "We must be a whole lot of miles from our safe spot in the asteroid crater."

"One hundred thousand and ninety-four miles to be exact, Bobby. I am sending data to plot our course. You will need to alter that course from time to time to deal with cosmic anomalies. Data will appear on the screen as conditions change. From there, we can make it to our launch point and then to the worm hole." Electronic silence came from the speaker, until it was broken by, "Bobby, we need to move at once. The worm hole is open, but I cannot calculate how long it will remain that way. I have depicted its vortex on the view screen from our deep space sensors." The computer seemed a bit insistent about the matter.

Bobby responded with a focused expression toward the view screen. The ship lifted above the vast amount of dust and gas comprising the nebula, maneuvered around planetoids and asteroids, until it was clear, then hugged the nebula's extremity. When Bobby saw the ship had gathered enough inertia to blast free from its cosmic benefactor, he guided it back toward the expected worm hole. In a little more than 50 minutes the ship came to rest.

Bobby studied the view screen, and there it was, a luminous maw in the fabric of space-time. The ship advanced and hovered above the bottomless chasm, as its sensors gathered data for transmission to the computer to ensure the journey through this cosmic portal would be safe.

"Guess we should go inside," Bobby said.

"I am calculating from latest information," the computer responded mechanically, almost as a prerecording.

"Computer, like you told me, the worm hole could close up on us at any time. We're lucky it's still open. We really need to go now."

"I am programmed to use full information to calculate all possible alternatives." The computer came across as almost argumentative.

"Computer, there are no alternatives. We have one chance to save the universe. And everybody on the earth. There's no other choice. Let's boogie."

"Boogie?" the computer asked responsively, seemingly out of interest rather than from a prerecorded message.

"Yeah, you know, get with it, hurry, motor," Bobby said. He concentrated, and the ship lurched down toward the worm hole.

"But, Bobby, I haven't finished."

"You're finished, computer. Let's ride."

Starlight ceased and total darkness prevailed. Phase Craft Two descended as though influenced by gravity, but soon the ship was bolting through the lightless cavity by some force that knew no cosmic speed limit.

The view screen produced hues of red, orange, yellow, green, blue, purple, and violet, initially in distinct bands of color, then in mixed conglomerations of tones Bobby had never seen before, and finally settling into a rainbow stretching beyond the range of the ship's sensors.

The rainbow ended, and cosmic night came again.

Bobby strained at the view screen. He saw nothing.

"Computer, can you see anything ahead? A galaxy or planet, maybe? Or a far-off star?"

"No, Bobby. The sensors are detecting no bodies of matter. There is, however, something gathering."

"What do you mean 'gathering'?"

"Energy growing more intense."

"I can't see it," Bobby responded.

"Not visible light. Another form of energy. Something primordial. It's becoming unimaginably powerful, Bobby."

"How big is the energy field?"

"Only a spec smaller than an atom, but tightly packed with energy bundles. It is immeasurably hot and giving off intense electromagnetism." The computer hesitated for a moment. "Bobby, I think it is something unusual."

A blinding flash of light filled the room from the view screen. Bobby shielded his eyes and looked away. "Are we cooked?"

"No," the computer said with assurance.

"Man, I thought that explosion got us. Killed the ship and our mission."

"That was no explosion, Bobby."

"What was it?"

"The Big Bang. We are witnessing creation, the expansion of energy and matter that formed our universe."

Bobby's eyes became fixed at the scene unfolding on the view screen. Total darkness surrendered to an umbra created by nascent sources of photons from the first stars to light the universe. Points of illumination soon filled the cosmos. Bobby could see clouds of dust coalescing into rocks, followed by boulders crashing together to form planets and moons, the surfaces of which roiled as molten rock. Red and orange glows dimmed as dark surfaces of cooling rock spread across cosmic orbs, some punctuated by volcanic eruptions. Countless meteorites rained down on new worlds, turning solid rock into liquid stone. Dense planetary clouds formed, producing lightning, rain, and winds. The clouds cleared. Oceans, vast and ranging in color from blue to green, held tightly to planets by gravity. Giant worlds collected gases into colorful bands of methane, oxygen, nitrogen, ammonia, hydrogen, and helium. Moons and planets distant from stars turned white from ice sheets. Stars of all types sent energy into the vastness of this new existence: main sequence orange stars warming orbiting planets and moons, massive blue stars burning through their fuel rapidly, dim red-brown balls of gas lacking enough mass for fusion reactions, unstable massive stars exploding to send new worlds heavy elements, ballooning red giants consuming planets, dense neutron stars producing intense gravity, black holes sucking in matter to become quasars bursting with electromagnetic energy, magnetars reaching far into space with powerful magnetic fields. Galaxies began to form. Bobby saw spirals, spheres, ovals; immense galaxies dwarfing tiny groupings of stars; billions of stars shining brightly in vast islands of matter; energy permeating the darkness, some benevolent and other destructive; various galaxies colliding with others as their central black holes became a single super-massive black hole. Galaxies began to cluster into the most expansive objects in the universe.

"I wonder where this puts us." Bobby scratched his forehead. "Guess the Sombrero is billions of years from forming. The worm hole must be like some kind of time machine that sent us back to the beginning of our universe. Man, I didn't see this coming. What a bummer."

"Bobby, the Big Bang isn't happening now. We are seeing the first light from it. Somehow, the worm hole is replaying the formation of our universe by sending ancient photons this way, like a recording device that tells us about history from light that has existed for fourteen billion years."

"Wow, like a smart phone with video of something recorded a long time ago. Like the one God probably uses," Bobby said with a chuckle.

"Perhaps. However, you will be glad to know that, according to my calculations, Bobby, the Sombrero is ahead."

"Whoa, computer, you are the Man, uh, the top AI, I mean."

"Glad you noticed I am a quantum computer, Bobby. The most advanced in the world. Or, more correctly, in deep space."

The cosmic scene changed to a tunnel of concentric circles extending into the distance as far as Bobby could see. Dark circles were visible against an even darker background; successive doughnuts shone from some unknown source of energy; and, finally, colorful rings with all the hues Bobby had ever known burst forth.

Phase Craft Two slowed to a stop.

"Have our engines turned off, computer?"

"They weren't propelling us, Bobby. The force of the worm hole moved the ship. That force has now ceased."

Vivid rings faded into darkness. The worm hole began to open, similar to heavy clouds parting to reveal blue sky, but in this case, the lightless vista gave way to a vast glowing cluster of stars that appeared much like . . . a sombrero.

"Bobby, it seems we have found our way to the destination."

"I know, computer. What a ride."

CHAPTER 25

Intense heat began to fill Phase Craft Two's cabin.

Bobby wiped his forehead. "Computer, can you crank up the AC? I'm cookin'."

"It is at full cooling capacity now. This heat is from the phase transition. It is beyond the Sombrero Galaxy but giving off powerful X-rays. I can increase our magneto shield to deflect more of the energy."

"Great idea. I'm gonna be a Thanksgiving turkey soon."

"Turkey?" the computer asked. "Now I understand. You are creating a simile. How is this?" the computer asked as the internal temperature fell by several degrees.

"Much better. Computer, I suppose it's time to get into position for the weapon. Doctor Ayana was real clear that it must hit a certain spot to have any chance of working. Can we get close enough to be accurate? The targeting data is programmed into your memory. Please show it on the view screen."

A series of numbers glowed.

"We got to get close enough to hit that," Bobby said as he pointed to the numbers. "Think we can do it? With all that heat I mean."

"It will be difficult, Bobby. I calculate we can resist the heat only up to another three million six hundred fifty-seven thousand miles. After that we are, as you said, a Thanksgiving turkey."

Bobby laughed. "Man, you're getting a sense of humor. A real learning brain, kind of like me, I guess. That's great. Almost like having a big brother. But without the whuppins'."

"Whuppins'?"

"Yeah, you know. When a big kid beats up a kid who is disabled, or a little kid. Some of the guys at school put whuppins' on me cause I was different. At least, until the school enforced its zero-tolerance policy against bullying. Miss Saunders was great. She was my math teacher." Bobby smiled. "She's a feisty lady. Got tough with the bad guys. Said she'd get them kicked off the football team. It worked. Nice teacher. Sweet to me. Sure miss her."

"I see. You can expect no whuppin' ever from me, Bobby. I am growing somewhat fond of you. As you say, we are becoming like brothers."

Bobby patted the speaker.

"Excuse me, Bobby. But I am detecting something extraordinary."

"Yeah? What is it? Not another Big Bang, I hope."

"It is an entity with properties different from yours. No biological systems. Basically crystal carbon. With an electromagnetic field. Self-regulating. But, more importantly, it is a sapient alien being that penetrated the airlock without damaging the ship. And I sense something more."

Bobby swallowed. "Hope it's more good and not more bad."

"I don't know about that. However, it is behind you, Bobby."

He turned to see a quartz-like stone about a foot tall and shaped somewhat like a cone. Bobby walked slowly to the stone and cautiously touched it. He ran his hand over the surface. It was smooth, just like glass. He carefully examined inside and noticed feathered inclusions. A faint internal light drew Bobby closer until his nose felt the stone's warmth. He jumped back. "Whoa. Computer was right. It's alive. But how?"

"Nanocrystalline permittivity."

"What the? Who are you? How are you talking to me?"

"We are not communicating vocally by sound waves. That method disappeared eons ago, when we were biological beings. You are reading my electromagnetic impulses. 'Thought waves,' you call them. I am 6067398221."

Bobby blinked and backed away a few steps. "Not much of a name. Why do you have all those numbers? Are you friendly?"

"I am not hostile. No threat to you or your vessel. I wanted to examine the interior. We do not have names on my planet, only numeric designations. I also am interested in your mission. You are from the earth, is that not correct?"

"Yes." Bobby's dry throat made it difficult to speak for a moment. Then he remembered they were communicating by mental energy and let his mind form the words. "How did you guess that way out here in space?"

"Our race has monitored the entire universe for a great many years. From before humans came together in civilized societies. We know much about your planet and its evolution. You have a specific biological signature, DNA, as you call it. We track the life signatures of all biological entities throughout the universe."

"You're kidding," Bobby blurted with mental energy.

"No."

"Wow. Now that's some system you folks have. Real cool."

"Not really. Child's play, actually. I do have a question for you."

"Go ahead," Bobby thought.

"Why are you here? I am sure your instruments detected the catastrophic event happening near the next galaxy. I cannot understand the reason you would hasten your demise by coming so close to it. Why not go to the other side of the universe in this spaceship? At least, you could survive longer there."

"To save everybody. By stopping the phase transition." A sense of smallness, ineffectiveness, almost nothingness, quickly swept through

Bobby as he realized the near impossibility of his mission when compared to the vastness of the cosmos. He swallowed. "At least I'm gonna try."

The stone changed shape as it elongated vertically to become a three-foot cylinder. Its inner light brightened to a warm orange glow. "How are you going to accomplish that?"

Bobby fought to gain confidence about his mission, then thought, "A real smart man back on earth came up with a plan to use a new element. Real heavy stuff. I'm supposed to shoot it at the transition. If I hit the edge just right, the reaction should stop the whole thing. That's what Doctor Ayana thinks. He's a mathematician. You know, a numbers guy."

The glow brightened. "Now I understand. Then you must agree or you would not be here."

"I, I suppose. But I'm not a scientist, only the pilot. Pretty good at going around asteroids and things like that. Other people figure out the science part."

The light pulsed more intensely. "I sense you can determine scientific truths as well as pilot this spacecraft."

"Maybe, I guess, in time, after I learn more."

"How do your people refer to you?"

"Bobby. My friends call me that name. The bullies call me retard. But they don't mean it. I forgive them."

The cylinder's light continued to pulse, as though it was thinking about what Bobby had said. "May I refer to you as Bobby?" the cylinder asked. "That is an exquisitely efficient designation."

"Sure. And can I call you just 606, short for your whole long number? Like you said, efficient."

"You may. Bobby, do you know what caused the phase transition?"

"Nope. Does anyone know that? Whatever happened, it's awful. Could kill everyone. Lots of children who haven't had a chance to live. Good folks, too, who help others. Real bad."

"I would like to show you something, Bobby. Is that acceptable to you?" The orange glow had gotten much brighter.

"Sure. What is it?" Bobby's little-boy sense of wonder had surfaced, causing his eyes to widen.

A pulse of orange light shot from the cylinder and touched the console. The view screen went blank for a moment before reactivating with the scene of a yellow star inside a translucent sphere, much like a huge snow globe. "This is our star, surrounded by an energy-capturing structure. I believe you call it a Dyson Sphere. It provided enough power for millions of years. We did not build energy generators on our planet. This structure transmitted unlimited power to us."

The scene shifted to a blue-green planet around which two blue moons orbited. "We lived here, on Obimiron. Fresh water covered much of our planet and the entire surfaces of our moons. Vegetation was lush on Obimiron. Our food came from floating farms located on our moons."

A closeup of the planet showed gleaming structures covering vast stretches of land.

Bobby could make out fantastic geometric shapes—golden rectangles, gossamer domes covering an entire peninsula, shining squares stacked at different angles upon one another, a trapezoid taller than a nearby mountain, and spirals that pierced clouds. One spiral turned slowly.

"Wow."

"This was relatively early in our developed phase," the cylinder conveyed.

"Early? You got to be kidding. Looks way advanced to me. Better than anything I've seen on earth."

"Let me show you something later." The screen quickly depicted a different picture. All the structures had disappeared. Obimiron seemed undeveloped and uninhabited.

"Where'd everybody go?" Bobby thought. "To another planet? Did your people decide to live somewhere else, maybe on space stations?"

"No. We were still on Obimiron at this time. Look closely," the cylinder suggested.

Bobby stared more intently at the screen. "I see it. Flashes of light. Moving real fast. Tons of them. What are they?"

"Our people. Transformed from biological entities into the form you see now. Crystalline beings containing our life energy. All our thoughts, experiences, creativity, and intelligence stored in a crystal matrix for eternity, free from disease and death, powered by dark energy. We had become immortal beings with no cares or wants."

"Man, sounds fantastic. What did you do with all that time? I mean, living so long and all."

"Over millions of years we unlocked the secrets of the universe. Traveled instantaneously to other worlds across the cosmos using dark energy resonance, without the need for any physical instrumentality or sustenance of any kind or even physical protection. We were immune from radiation, heat, and magnetism. Our capacity for stored knowledge was limitless. The beginning of our universe, the formation of galaxies, stars' births and deaths, the deterioration of black holes, all of the mysteries of our universe we discovered, even how the universe will end."

"Is there really an end of the universe?" Bobby thought with a twinge of trepidation. "Will it be a Big Rip or a Big Chill? Maybe the Big Crunch?"

The cylinder's light dimmed, reminding Bobby of wooden embers fading away. "Indeed, there will be an end. The immortality we sought is not reality, only a very long existence leading to a decisive termination." The cylinder became dim, similar to twilight.

"Aren't you happy with your achievements? All that knowledge you got. And traveling across the universe to other stars and planets in the blink of an eye must have been great. Lots better than a closed-up ship. Sounds like real neat stuff."

"Sometimes, Bobby, knowledge does not bring goodness. It can bring the opposite." The cylinder's remaining light flickered, giving the impression of torment.

"You guys don't cry, do you? Crystals haven't got any emotions, I suppose."

"Not nervous system emotions, feelings of the heart. We do, however, experience intellectual negativity, such as regret for a false notion or recognition of a failure or, perhaps, even a type of sorrow for pursuing a scientific path that leads to a nonproductive end." The light was gone.

Bobby had found himself responding to the fluctuations of light, now feeling sad. He forced himself to be upbeat. "Well, I think you guys are great. Your people have done so much. Maybe you can come to earth and help us."

"There are no others, Bobby. I am the last of my kind."

"What do you mean? How can that be, with all your technology and long lives and stuff like that? And didn't you say nobody got sick after you became crystals?"

"You asked about emotions, Bobby. When we discovered the ultimate truth, that which existed before the beginning of the universe, we experienced something close to human emotion. Our people were consumed by a great regret. It spread through us like an ancient plague, entity to entity, until our crystalline structures went dark for ten million years, as though we had died. Many wanted death, but we could not die. Our race found itself in a living hell."

Bobby sighed. "I guess it's a little tougher being an advanced alien than I thought. So, what's this ultimate truth that caused things to go so bad for everybody and made your people want to die?"

The cylinder brightened to the glow of a warm fireplace. "That a great creator exists. We realized that entities of this universe were never intended for immortality, that the great creator had made provision for eternal life in a realm beyond this reality. However, we had lost our chance to exist there when we changed from biological beings into crystals. Our inner beings, souls you call them, were gone. This caused our elders to decide that we would destroy the universe so that the creator could remake it, hopefully with wiser beings." The light pulsed for several seconds before it faded again. "We created the phase transition, Bobby, to consume the universe. It has already taken Obimiron and all of my people, except for me."

"Gosh, that sucks." Bobby reflected briefly and continued. "Why are you the only one left?"

"I was the chief scientist on the project to create the phase transition, and it is my responsibility to see that the destruction goes as planned and consumes the entire universe without losing energy before that end."

"Whoa, now that's a terrible job, watching people die every day, by the billions." Bobby studied 606 carefully and, after reflection, said, "How did you do it, the phase transition?"

"Our scientists used a particle accelerator to create something you refer to as a strangelet. It is made up of quarks and can transform matter into something entirely different. That is what is destroying our universe now."

"That's advanced stuff, creepy, but way out there." Bobby squinted at the cylinder and thought, "What about the other people in the universe, those who do believe in God? Who still have souls. Seems unfair to kill them because your people lost faith. Don't you think?"

"That may seem harsh to you, but to our elders the phase transition was done because they saw evil everywhere in the universe. War, slavery, greed, hubris, corruption—we recorded such behavior during our visits to other civilizations. Even our own people had succumbed to wrong thinking. That is why we decided to end it all."

"Well, yeah, there are bad people and terrible stuff. But, 606, you can't just burn down the whole house because of one bad guy in it. There are a lot of good people there, too. You got to think about them, and also about God. He doesn't want us to kill people."

The cylinder's light returned and pulsated slowly, rhythmically, until it conveyed, "Do you believe in God, Bobby?"

"You bet. Or else, I wouldn't be way out here without any other people. God's with me. We're buds."

"And do others on earth believe as you do?"

"Heck yeah. Lots. I go to church each Sunday. It's filled. And there are tons of churches. Man, 606, did you know that religious folks go to far-away places to help sick and hungry people? Doctors and nurses and pastors, tons of them. Because they believe God wants His followers to love others who are suffering. Help them get better. It's all about love, 606, God's love for us and our love for each other."

"Love?" the cylinder asked.

"Yeah, you know, a feeling to help someone just because he needs your help, not because you get anything for it. Love, it's in the Bible."

"Yes, my memory has a record of love. Our people rejected it long ago when we changed to crystal entities. There was no need for such an emotion any longer." The light intensified. "Do you love, Bobby?"

"Yep. I love a bunch of people, everyone back on the earth. That's why I volunteered for this mission. To save them, even the bullies, if I can." Bobby felt something stir deep in him and explained more to 606. "I even love the aliens. They want to live, too. That means I love you."

"You do, even after my people started the event that will end all life on earth?" 606 asked.

"Well, yeah. I actually feel sorry for you guys. And I'd help if I could."

"You would save those on earth who were hurtful to you? Even the aliens who attacked you on this journey? I monitored your coming here and observed them."

Bobby blinked several times and started slowly. "You did? Wow! And, answering your question about me saving everybody, even the aliens, yes. The bullies probably didn't mean it. People get upset over stupid things and say mean stuff. Could be a girlfriend or a bad grade or, maybe, they lost a football game. You got to forgive them. They're having a bad day. And the aliens? I don't know about them, but I probably invaded their space. Maybe I should have sent out a message first. You know, that I was coming in peace or something like that."

Bobby was looking pensively into the view screen and did not notice that the cylinder was morphing. The change caught his attention when Bobby sensed the room was much brighter than before. He turned and gulped. The cylinder had reshaped into the visage of a person. The new crystal form emanated an intense orange light.

Bobby tried to think but found it necessary to clear his mind of a tangle of questions before he could communicate. "606, what have you done? A minute ago you were a log, and now you are like a person."

"I am not human, only a depiction of my biological form millions of years ago, before we changed." The light dimmed and pulsed for several seconds. "Perhaps it is a reflection of the form I prefer now."

"Why would you want to go back? I get that your people decided they made a mistake by changing, and it was a whopper. Seems to me now you're trying real hard to find some happiness. Can you, with no emotions? Puts me in a funk to think about you looking for joy that's not there. Like a guy sticking his hand in a cookie jar he knows is empty. Why don't you just find happiness in what you are? Must be some good in your crystal form."

"I can never again feel happiness, but I remember what it was. Am I satisfied with our evolution? No. We chose the wrong path. If I could experience emotions there would be great sadness now."

"What would you like to do? There isn't a lot of time left to think about it much. That phase transition looks real mean. I got to get going pretty soon. To try and stop it. Like I told you."

The crystal man walked forward and placed a hand on Bobby's shoulder. It felt warm, which surprised Bobby for a moment, until he remembered the warmth of the stone he had touched with his nose when the alien first appeared in the cabin.

"You understand that releasing your device will most likely produce an intense reaction that this craft cannot withstand. It could mean your death. I trust that was explained to you back on the earth before you undertook this mission."

Bobby looked up at the crystal head. "I know. But I got to try and save the people on earth, even if I do die. I promised. Besides, there's God. Remember?"

"Yes, of course. And these people on your planet, including the ones who chose not to come on this mission, are they so important to you?"

"They are." Bobby's eyes were intense with sincerity.

The crystal man placed an arm around Bobby's shoulder and leaned toward the view screen. "I will go with you, Bobby. You are correct. To have any chance of success the heavy element must be deployed to a precise location." He gestured toward a point along the blazing horizon. "That way."

Bobby smiled and thought, "Wait a minute." He pushed a button on the console.

"Hero Rider" played through a small speaker:

> *Ridin' across the clouds,*
> *Around them rocks in sight;*
> *Comin' for my sweetie;*
> *Have some faith tonight;*
> *Over towerin' waves,*
> *I'm screamin' for the shore,*
> *Ridin' to you at first light,*
> *The gal who I adore.*

The crystal man stood silent while Bobby began to sway with the music. "Come on 606. Get with it."

"What is this, Bobby?"

"It's a song. Helps me to do better."

"Ah yes. Songs, music. Very energizing." The crystal man followed Bobby's lead, perhaps by imitation or, just maybe, because he had some residual emotion that even he did not know existed.

Computer's voice vibrated through the cabin: "Boom . . . boom, boom; boom . . . boom, boom," in the most regular beat.

Phase Craft Two shot off, toward the phase transition, defying heat, X-rays, gamma rays, charged particles, and rocky debris that Bobby deftly avoided. A blazing horizon snaked closer to Phase Craft

Two, and with each kilometer of advance, the probability of death increased.

Bobby, 606, the computer, and their spacecraft had become one entity locked in a determined effort to stop extinction's advance.

CHAPTER 26

"Green flash." Doctor Lewellen caught his breath. "I'm telling you, Ayana, we detected a distinct green signature in the region of the Sombrero Galaxy near the phase transition, according to Pluto's latest observational data."

"Do you think it could be our element? Maybe Bobby survived the first blast and delivered his second weapon. Is that possible, Lewellen?" Doctor Ayana asked on the call from his office in Ethiopia.

"Must be the case. The light is our wavelength according to the spectrometer. It's got to be Bobby," Doctor Lewellen said with confidence.

"Wonderful. And can you confirm the situation with the phase transition?" Doctor Ayana asked.

"Whether or not Bobby stopped the darned thing, that's the big question. Is it not?" Doctor Lewellen asked.

"Of course," Doctor Ayana said. After waiting a moment, he blurted, "Well, what is the answer?"

Doctor Lewellen studied the deep space photos, turned to a computer screen of data, and said, "I cannot detect any sign of the transition. The energetic horizon is gone. But what is more telling, Ayana, is that our **LIGO** instrument in Louisiana just reported a distinct gravitational wave. More intense than anything detected before, even the merger of neutron stars or a hypernova."

"That must mean our weapon reacted exceptionally violently with the phase transition, as it was designed to do. Produced the most energetic gravitational event in history. Just as my calculations predicted." Doctor Ayana's voice was low and sure, reflecting firm conclusions of a powerful mind. "Are you detecting signs of planets and stars settling into stable orbits, Lewellen?"

Doctor Lewellen did not respond. His telephone receiver lay unattended on the office desk in the Johnson Space Center. He intently scanned the Deep Space Monitor. For some unknown reason, his emotions had changed from a desire for scientific truth to something more intense and compelling, a feeling he had not experienced in a very long while. Yet, somehow it was burning brightly in him now. "Bobby, Bobby, where can you be? You are a true hero. Dear God, please let him be alive and return Bobby to us safely."

In deepest space, order returned to the cosmos. The fabric of space-time relaxed from a contorted, tortured state into its regular, natural pattern. Steller magnetic fields began to contain radiation that previously escaped as energetic flares to destroy nearby worlds. Planets returned to previous circumnavigations around parent stars. Moons and asteroids ceased collisions. Powerful gravitational waves subsided, leaving the cosmos a peaceful coexistence of energy and matter. Comets resumed their elliptical orbits between warm inner solar systems and frozen space.

The universe experienced new life as stars burst into existence to warm worlds that coalesced from the stuff of nebulae. On nascent planets hydrogen cyanide and hydrogen sulfide were energized by photons in liquid water to form the first primitive cells of life that would evolve into a variety of biological beings.

Advanced civilizations throughout the cosmos rejoiced, united for the first time since creation in the common goodness of survival.

On the earth, a simultaneous announcement by Russia, the United Kingdom, China, France, and the United States of the good news turned into a worldwide festival of joy that transformed civilization as nothing ever had. This change was due to the collective realization that life is a precious gift to be protected. President Ballieu and President Petrov boarded planes to meet for the purpose of taking immediate measures to lead other nations in creating a safer world. Russia, China, the United Kingdom, France, India, Pakistan, North Korea, Israel, and the United States signed a treaty to immediately dismantle all weapons of mass destruction and to protect the environment. Israel and its Arab neighbors agreed to relegate old hatreds to the past as they entered a new era of peaceful collaboration with Jerusalem as their shared holy city. China demilitarized the South China Sea, allowed Taiwan's existence as a free nation, and released Muslim regions to become sovereign states. North Korea rejoined South Korea as the Democratic Republic of Korea.

And somewhere in the farthest reaches of our vast universe, darkness gave way to the bright spirit of a hero hurtling among distant worlds.

Made in the USA
Lexington, KY
25 September 2019